James Philip

After Midnight

UNTIL THE NIGHT – BOOK FIVE

Copyright © James P. Coldham writing as James Philip, in respect of After Midnight, Book 5 of the Until the Night Series (the serialisation of the 2nd Edition of Until the Night), 2016.
All rights reserved.

Cover concept by James Philip
Graphic Design by Beastleigh Web Design

The Bomber War Series

Book 1: Until the Night
Book 2: The Painter
Book 3: The Cloud Walkers

Until the Night Series

A serialisation of Book 1: Until the Night in five parts

Part 1: Main Force Country – September 1943
Part 2: The Road to Berlin – October 1943
Part 3: The Big City – November 1943
Part 4: When Winter Comes – December 1943
Part 5: After Midnight – January 1944

After Midnight

I do not personally regard the whole of the remaining cities of Germany as worth the bones of one British Grenadier. It therefore seems to me that there is one and only one valid argument on which a case for giving up strategic bombing could be based, namely that it has already completed its task and that nothing now remains for the Armies to do except to occupy Germany against unorganized resistance.

Air Marshall Sir Arthur Harris
[Air Officer Commanding-in-Chief RAF Bomber Command]

Chapter 1

Saturday 1st January, 1944
The Rectory, Ansham Wolds, Lincolnshire

The Lancaster passed almost directly over the Rectory. Eleanor leaned over the sink and watched the bomber through the kitchen window as it droned on down the valley, swiftly disappearing into the murk and the falling snow. The overnight snowfall carpeted the hillside and several boys from the village were noisily – when they were not exchanging volleys of snowballs - clearing the path up to the church.

The Lancasters had been taking off and landing for the last hour or so. Test flights, the prelude to a raid. She wondered if Adam would be flying tonight, tried to put the thought out of her mind. She had not seen him since Thursday evening. Yesterday, she had celebrated New Year's Eve with Simon and Adelaide Naismith-Parry. Adelaide was unwell, the cold was a great trial to her but thankfully, Simon had shaken off his recent bronchitis and was restored to something like his best form. The old couple had been delighted when she broke her good news. Had it not been for Adelaide's arthritis Eleanor suspected the Rector and his wife would have danced a jig of delight in her honour.

Adam had left it to her to make a start on the necessary arrangements. No sooner had he proposed and she accepted than he had fled back to his Squadron. He said he was concerned for her reputation and would not be persuaded that his worries were unfounded. Bless him. He worried overmuch about such silly things.

Eleanor had arranged for Simon to read the wedding banns over the next three Sundays. Although no date for the wedding had yet been set, two dates - both Saturdays - were under consideration, the 22nd and the 29th January but nothing could be settled until Adam next dragged himself away from the station.

"We'd like the wedding to be as soon as possible," she had explained to the Rector. "I hope people won't think that's wrong coming so soon after father's death?"

"This is wartime," the old man reminded her, smiling. "Nobody will think any the worse of you. Quite the contrary, I should imagine. Have you made any plans for the honeymoon?"

"Goodness, no!" Eleanor admitted, flustered without knowing why. "To be absolutely honest, we haven't discussed much of anything, actually."

Now, as another Lancaster rumbled low over the tower of St. Paul's church, Eleanor's thoughts were restless. Her initial excitement was undimmed, but worrisome practicalities had begun to jostle for her attention.

The Rector came into the kitchen. "There seems to be a lot of activity this afternoon?"

"Another big raid, probably."

The old man agonised for a moment: "I should imagine Adam must be due for a rest soon?"

Eleanor half-turned to look at him.

"If he is, he's not mentioned it, Simon."

"No," he smiled. "The Wing-Commander would

make a formidable poker player. He likes to keep his cards close to his chest. Group Captain Alexander once told me that six months in charge of a squadron is a very good stint. Quite apart from the number of ops a chap flies. My understanding is that your young man is due for a rest on both counts. As I say, presumably fairly soon."

Eleanor returned to the pans in the sink. It went without saying that she longed for the day when Adam stopped flying ops. The trouble was, when that day came, the RAF could send him anywhere. He had warned her that 'the strict letter' of Kings Regulations prevented a man being posted to a station less than forty miles distant from his wife. He might be sent overseas. They could be separated for years. She had begun to prepare herself for the worst, stoically consoling herself that the war would not last forever.

"My young man, indeed!" She chided the Rector. "There's life in me yet, you know!"

"Forgive me, my dear," the old man protested, deeply troubled lest he had given even the slightest of offence. "I didn't mean to suggest…"

"I know you didn't, Simon," she laughed. Adam was six years her junior and although he seemed indifferent to the fact, privately she was less sanguine. Then there were the children. How did he really feel about bringing up another man's son and daughter?

"I talk too much," confessed the Rector.

Eleanor wiped her hands on her apron, touched the old man's arm.

"No you don't. I know you're trying to be kind."

"I'm sure everything will be fine."

"Of course it will be," she scolded him, her brown eyes twinkling. "Now you must go back to your study, Simon. Tea will be late if you don't stop distracting me."

The Rector beat a hasty retreat.

Eleanor's thoughts roamed across the changed landscape of her life as she assembled cups, saucers, plates and cutlery from the old oak cupboards beside the sink. It had cost Adam a great deal to confess his affair with Helen Fulshawe, to lay bare his soul to her and to confess to his darkest secret.

'It's over!' He had said.

That was all she needed to know.

Chapter 2

Saturday 1st January, 1944
RAF Ansham Wolds, Lincolnshire

The Lancaster Force had been briefed for Berlin; on the first day of the New Year there could be no other target.

The crews were braced for the signal to start up when the first postponement clattered up on the Operations Room teleprinter. Take off had been scheduled for eight o'clock and initially, it was put back an hour. The crews had stayed in their aircraft: fretting in the cold, whiling away the minutes, waiting, waiting. Then the off was postponed again, indefinitely.

The mood in the Operations Room was restive, especially when it became apparent that the original operations plan took no account of the extremely strong westerly tail winds predicted in the latest forecast.

"Right." Adam decided, rising from the Operations Room chair in which he had been dozing. He made no attempt to conceal his disenchantment. "This has gone on long enough! Get the chaps out of their kites. Let's have the crew buses out to the dispersals. Everybody back to the ready room. Somebody warn the NAAFI to lay on hot drinks and sandwiches. Now! Chop! Chop!"

Around him the Operations Staff jumped – they literally 'jumped' - into action. Chairs scraped loudly, orders were barked, phones were snatched up, people scurried for the exit.

"And get me Group on the scrambler line!"

There was nothing worse than a postponement, except that is, a second postponement. At least when an op was scratched at the last minute the crews knew that was that and they could relax and put the awfulness of it behind them for another night.

"The Operations Officer is in conference, sir," apologised a nervous WAAF, after a short delay.

Adam grunted. Freddie Tomlinson lacked Pat Farlane's appetite for a shouting match. More than one irate Squadron Commander would be demanding to bend his ear. He took the receiver.

"To whom am I speaking to?"

It turned out he was talking to Freddie Tomlinson's deputy, an unflappable squadron leader in his late forties who had, reputedly, flown as an air observer/gunner in the C-in-C's Squadron in Iraq in the twenties. Bob Tufnell was a hard man to have a row with, he never rose to the bait, met every slingshot with unfailing civility and infuriating good humour. Which was probably why in Freddie Tomlinson's absence he had been nominated to field the worst of the flak from the Group's most irate station and Squadron Commanders.

"What the bloody hell's going on, Bob?" Adam demanded, irascibly. "My chaps have been hanging around for over an hour now. It's not good enough!"

"I'm dreadfully sorry, sir," replied the other man, his voice squeaky, distorted by the line. "The Ops Officer is presently in with the AOC, so is the

Nav Officer, I gather. It's this damned met forecast. The wires have been burning red hot between here and Command."

Adam heard him out. He would have interrupted Freddie Tomlinson, but then Freddie would have expected him to interrupt.

"Oh, for goodness sake! You're not telling me they're having second thoughts about the route, Bob?"

"Sorry, sir. I couldn't say, sir."

Adam hung up.

"Any news yet?" Ben Hardiman inquired, sauntering into the Operations Room, stifling a yawn.

"It sounds like they're thinking of changing the route."

The big man frowned and looked at the clock on the wall.

"If they don't make up their minds soon," he said, rubbing his chin, "we'll have to go straight in and straight out, anyway. If they want to go at all tonight, that is."

Adam dug out his cigarettes.

The original route sent the Lancaster Force on a northerly track across the German Bight, into Schleswig-Holstein and over the Baltic between Flensburg and Kiel. Twenty miles north of Fehmarn the route turned south-east and arrowed directly for the German capital. The route avoided known flak concentrations and kept well to the north of the night fighters' favourite hunting grounds over the plains of Saxony but nobody had pretended it was perfect.

'I don't like the long leg south-east,' Mac had

declared. 'A hundred and ninety miles on a constant bearing from Fehmarn to the target is asking for trouble. Once the openers have passed south of Rostock it's obvious where they're going.'

Adam had objected, albeit mildly, to this line or argument.

'If you were in the enemy's shoes, wouldn't you have a nasty suspicion Brunswick and Magdeburg were in the frame? Right up to the moment the first cookies went down in Berlin?'

Mac was in a huff. He and his crew were off to the Pathfinders in the morning and he had wanted to sign off on a high note with a trip to the Big City. Adam had forbidden him to fly that night. Just to be sure he had assigned Mac's Lancaster, K-King, to another crew.

Mac would forgive him, eventually.

'Look, sir,' the Scot had pleaded, quietly determinedly and very earnestly. 'This means a lot to me. And to the chaps, too. Will you not reconsider?'

Adam had almost weakened. Mac had been his staunchest ally at Ansham Wolds in those early days. If his was the face of 647 Squadron, then Mac had always been its hard-working, press on beating heart.

'No, Mac. I will not reconsider my decision.' As an additional precaution he had asked Ben to make absolutely sure Mac kept his feet firmly on the ground until the Squadron was airborne.

"What have you done with Mac?" He asked the big man.

"I took him to the Mess and poured a couple of stiff drinks down his neck."

"Good idea."

Ben chuckled.

"What's so funny?" Growled Group Captain Alexander, peeling off his greatcoat and scarf. He had been under the weather again that day. Now he coughed asthmatically, produced a fresh large chequered handkerchief and blew his nose. His face was blotchy, his eyes streaming from walking in the cold outside.

"Er, nothing, sir."

"It's starting to snow again, by the way." Alexander sneezed. The flight surgeon had diagnosed bronchitis, made a series of loud clucking noises and prescribed aspirin and bed rest. The Old Man was having none of it. A touch of fever and a bad chest was not going to confine him to his bed and that was that. Not when there was an op on. "It's not good enough! Keeping the chaps hanging around like this!"

Behind the Station Commander the room was filling up. Everybody wanted to know what was going on, whether the crews would need to be re-briefed, or if the postponement was likely to become a cancellation.

"I've ordered the crews back to the ready room, sir."

"Good. What do Group say?"

"They aren't saying very much, sir. I think Command must be haggling with the Groups over a new route."

Ben cleared his throat.

"Something rather more direct, I should think, sir," he offered. "The new winds the met people are forecasting would have played merry hell with the old route. Particularly, that long last leg. If we go at all tonight, I suspect we'll go straight in."

"Dammit," Group Captain Alexander sighed. "If we don't go tonight, we could be snowed in for days. Days!"

Chapter 3

Sunday 2nd January, 1944
Lancaster R-Robert, 35 miles South of Berlin

Peter Tilliard was at pains to sound laconic as he called around the crew stations.

Tonight, was one of those ill-starred nights when everything went wrong and it was every man for himself. First there had been the postponements, then the change of route, a reversion to the 'normal' direct approach across Holland and northern Germany. Takeoff had been put back and put back again, eventually midnight had come and gone before they got off. Taking off between snow squalls was not his idea of good sport. Then, over Germany the clouds had stacked up, giant clouds the like of which he had never experienced. Raft upon raft of cloud, right up to twenty thousand feet. The fighters had got into the bomber stream over the Zuider Zee and distant combats had pursued R-Robert across northern Germany. Approaching Berlin the fighters danced in and out of the mountainous, towering thunderheads that snuffed out Sky Markers in a moment, turning the attack into a complete fiasco.

"Pilot to bomb-aimer. Did everything drop, Billy?"

"Yes, Skipper."

That was something.

There was no mistaking the release of a cookie - the aircraft soared, the controls became light and responsive - but there was always the chance one of the five hundred pounders might have hung up. On his first op at Ansham Wolds he had had a thousand pounder hang up. Not just any thousand pounder, but one fitted with a delayed action fuse set to detonate approximately eight hours after impact. No amount of diving and throwing the aircraft around had dislodged it. Over England they were diverted to an OTU field near Tetford, east of Lincoln where an Army Bomb Disposal unit had loaded the offending munition onto the back of a truck and whisked it off to a nearby quarry to blow it up. There was no safe way of finding out if a delayed action fuse had activated. Everybody hated delayed-action fuses.

"Pilot to W/T op. Still awake, George?"

"Yes, Skipper," answered the newest member of the crew. George Simpson was attempting to disentangle the snatches of German he was chasing around the frequencies. His pigeon German told him the enemy had not yet detected the bomber stream's southern path away from Berlin. From what little he could piece together, the night fighters were orbiting beacon Berta, west of the city. Tersely, he reported this to his pilot.

"Keep me informed," Tilliard acknowledged, tersely. "Out."

Jack Gordon, separated from the W/T operator in the mid-section of the fuselage by a blackout curtain, listened to the brief exchange. Yesterday afternoon he had found out the Skipper had discovered George's guilty secret: his history of malingering and back-sliding to avoid having to fly with sprogs.

'What do you think of George?' Peter Tilliard

had asked him, matter of factly, before the New Year's Eve celebrations began in earnest.

'He seems to know what he's about.' Jack had replied, guardedly. He himself had never been overly keen on flying with sprogs. Unless you trusted the chaps you were with, flying ops was miserable. George Simpson had slotted straight into the crew. He was every bit as sharp as poor dead Tom Dennison, probably better organised, much more the old lag. 'Keen as mustard.'

'That was my impression, too,' his friend had agreed, neutrally.

Jack was not going to get involved. Providing George Simpson pulled his weight, all well and good. If he let the side down then that was different. Until then he intended to give the man the benefit of the doubt and he hoped that was the way the Skipper would play it, too.

"Pilot to navigator. Wakey! Wakey!"

Jack grinned to himself, he could imagine the others smiling beneath their oxygen masks. The Skipper was in good form, he was always on his best form on a bad night.

"Ha! Ha!" He retorted. "Very funny!"

"How's the hangover, Jack?"

R-Robert's navigator had discovered early in his operational career that there was nothing quite like fear to remedy a thick head.

"Just fine and dandy, Skipper!"

Tilliard called up the gunners, exchanged short pleasantries with each and relinquished his monopoly of the intercom.

A little later flak lit the sky in the south.

"Chemnitz, Skipper," Jack Gordon reported,

plotting the range and bearing on his chart. "Somebody's got the winds wrong..."

Yes, Chemnitz...

The route home passed mid-way between Leipzig and Chemnitz. South-south-west of Leipzig, over Gera, the bomber stream would turn into the west, heading directly for the Cologne-Mainz gap. Tonight, flying into the teeth of the west wind it was going to be a long, long trip back and inevitably, many aircraft would be battered off course. If they were unlucky they would stray over one of the many hot spots to either side of the planned ground track. Jack checked and re-checked his calculations. The hurricane tail winds that had blown R-Robert the four hundred miles from the Dutch coast to Berlin in less than a hundred minutes had made accurate navigation a lottery. With a wind like that even a small error in the broadcast 'found winds' was a disaster. If that was Chemnitz down in the south then they were more or less on track; if, on the other hand...

If it was Leipzig, they were miles off course and they were in big trouble...

Leipzig?

No, it could not be Leipzig.

Surely not?

No...

"Shit!" He cursed under his breath, scrabbling urgently through his notes, trying to work backwards. "Shit! Shit! Shit!"

With nothing better to go on than a couple of wobbly star sights somewhere north of Hanover, and a great deal of wishful thinking about the accuracy of the Sky Markers they had bombed on over the Big City, R-Robert could very easily be miles off track.

Easily.

Fifty miles, sixty miles. Maybe more.

Jack swallowed hard, suddenly dry-mouthed as he fought down the panic.

"Navigator to pilot."

"Yes, Jack. What can I do for you?"

The Australian swallowed hard, again.

"Skipper, I don't think that's Chemnitz down in the south. I think it may be Leipzig."

There was a short silence, punctuated only by the hiss of the ether.

"Understood," Tilliard drawled, calmly, for all the world completely unconcerned. This was, after all, only a drive in the country on a sunny summer day. "If you think that's Leipzig, we'll give it a wide berth then, Jack. To the east?"

"Roger, Skipper. Come left to two-seven-oh."

"Two-seven-oh, roger."

Jack frantically updated his chart, redrew R-Robert's track. With a sinking heart he realised they had probably dropped their cookie, four 500-pounders and eight cans of incendiaries somewhere south of Potsdam into an area of lakes and forests some twenty miles south-east of the aiming point. He listened to the Skipper geeing up the gunners.

If they all got killed tonight it would be his fault.

Jack Gordon's fault.

Chapter 4

Sunday 2nd January, 1944
RAF Ansham Wolds, Lincolnshire

It was dark outside. Pitch black as snow flurried across the high wold. That afternoon the crews had sulkily flight tested their aircraft without ever really believing the Chief would actually send them out again that night. Most of the crews listed to fly tonight had participated in the previous night's Berlin operation, the majority not getting to bed until eight or nine that morning. Understandably, they were not overly impressed to be awakened two or three hours later with the news that ops were on again that night.

Work gangs had been clearing snow from the main runway all day. The gangs were still at work, sanding, gritting and salting the snow-free areas, and digging the flare path lights out of windblown drifts. The Squadron's Lancasters were being bombed up. In the next hour fuelling would begin.

Adam stepped up onto the low stage.

"Settle down, chaps!" He prefaced, clasping his trusty billiard cue. Normally, he would have left the preliminaries to the nominated briefing officer, let the Intelligence Officer and the other specialists get on with it. Normally, he would have contented himself with winding up the entertainment, and with offering a few words of wisdom to send the crews on their way. But today was not a normal day. Last night the Lancaster Force had lost 28 aircraft on the way to Berlin and although all

Ansham Wolds' heavies had returned, safe and sound bar a few flak marks, there was no doubt in his mind that the raid itself had been a complete shambles. Tonight, the Lancaster Force was being sent back to the Big City and as if this was not bad enough - and it was pretty bad - the Chief had decreed that, once again the bomber stream would fly the 'direct' route to Berlin. It had not taken Adam long to conclude that, all things considered, it would be best if he was the one who broke the news to the crews.

"Settle down!" He waited patiently for quiet. Turning to his left he addressed the WAAF at the side of the stage. The young woman was nervously holding the draw strings of the curtain covering the giant map of north-western Europe. "Carry on, please."

The curtain slid away to reveal the map.

Adam pursed his lips, scanned the faces before him as the initial groans threatened to turn into a groundswell of offended, angry dissent.

Anticipating the reaction of the crews Group Captain Alexander had attempted to rise from his sick bed, desperately keen to stand both morally and physically shoulder to shoulder with his Squadron Commander. Adam had quietly, stubbornly reassured him that this would not be necessary. The Old Man had taken a worrying turn for the worse overnight and the Flight Surgeon had called Adam to his bedside. The Station Master was running a dangerously high fever and pneumonia had taken hold.

'He ought to be transferred to a civilian hospital, in Hull or Lincoln,' had been the doctor's worried verdict. 'As soon as possible.'

Given that snow currently blocked the roads over the wold, this would not be practical until the morning at the earliest. Of course, the Old Man being the Old Man was more concerned about the coming operation than the trifling matter of his own welfare.

'The crews won't be very happy,' he had scowled, gasping for breath. 'But we can't have a scene. We mustn't let it get out of hand. These things are best nipped in the bud.'

'There won't be a scene, sir,' Adam had promised him.

Two hours ago he had telephoned Group Headquarters, spoken to the Deputy AOC, and made him aware of the seriousness of the Station Master's illness. Air Commodore Crowe-Martin had listened impassively, indicated that he would notify the AOC of the situation. An hour ago he had rung back. The Deputy Group Commander's orders had been succinct, practical and unambiguous.

'Until we know more about Alex's condition you will take over at Ansham Wolds. I shall rely on you to make sure Alex does what he's told. If the Flight Surgeon wants him in a proper hospital then he is to damn well go to a proper hospital. Soonest! As to the Squadron, do as you see fit in the interim. If you feel Bob Nicholson's ready, hand over the reins, now.'

Oddly, Adam found the idea of being in command of the whole station daunting in ways that commanding 647 Squadron in battle had never been. This briefing was his first test and he let the crews have their grumble. There were no catcalls, only whispers of discontent. Many commanding officers would have stamped on these murmurings but that was not his way. His crews were tired, they resented being asked to go straight back to the Big City. They were not fringe merchants, they were simply unhappy and – not to put too fine a point on it - they felt a little insulted. This was England, not Nazi Germany and *his* crews had a perfect right to grumble. He said nothing, waited, eying the faces of his crews. Presently, the muted rumblings subsided.

"Thank you, gentlemen," he said. "I realise that a lot of you were flying last night and that you are tired. Be that as it may be, we have a job to do. And we shall do it. In a moment the Intelligence Officer will give you the latest gen on the route and the aiming point. However, before we get down to tonight's show I have a couple of parish announcements." He paused. *Keep calm, keep things on an even keel. Business as usual.* "Squadron Leader McDonald has left us today for the Pathfinders. Mac's been a tower of strength on this Squadron. I would like to take this opportunity of wishing him well. I'm sure you will also." Mac had already gone; he and his old lags had flown down to Norfolk that morning. "Effective twelve hundred hours today Flight-Lieutenant Barlow has assumed command of A Flight."

Business as usual.

"You may be aware that Group Captain Alexander is currently under the weather. I'm sure he will be back on his feet in no time. However, for the next few days I shall be standing in for him as

Station Master. What this means is that *after* this evening's op, I shall be flying a desk until such time as Group Captain Alexander returns to duty. In the meantime Squadron Leader Nicholson will assume temporary command of 647 Squadron effective twelve hundred hours tomorrow."

He had taken Ben and the rest of the crew aside in the chilly, cluttered storeroom behind the stage twenty minutes before the briefing. The Groupie's indisposition had brought things forward, hastened the end of Adam's ops career and it was right and proper that the chaps were the first to hear. And hear it first from him.

'The Groupie's gone down with pneumonia, chaps. Which means I shall be stepping into his shoes pro tem. After tonight's op I probably won't be doing too many more ops. In fact, the way things are I may not do any more at all.' He allowed them a moment to digest this. When nobody said a word he went on. 'The way I see it is this. You chaps volunteered to come up here to fly with me. So, when I finish here, you will all be automatically screened. No ifs, no buts.'

Ben had lingered after the others were dismissed.

'Eleanor will be pleased.'

'I should think so, yes,' Adam had agreed, tersely.

He had warned the officers involved in tonight's briefing to keep to the script and to forget about jollying the crews along. The last thing his crews needed was to be 'jollied along' by a bunch of 'deskbound comedians'.

Tonight there was a possibility of severe icing

conditions and massive electrical storms on the outward route. In the past when such conditions had been forecast the Met Officer, a flabby, bespectacled man of about his own age, was wont to suggest to the crews they ought to be able to find 'safe avenues' through the worst storms. Which, of course, was abject nonsense.

'I don't want speculation. I want facts,' he had demanded, fixing the meteorologist in his stare. 'I expect you to tell my crews what's forecast. Not what Group think they should hear. You're answerable to me, not Group! Is that clear?'

'Yes, sir.'

At Waltham Grange Adam had acquired, some said cultivated, an evil reputation amongst the non-flying fraternity. At Ansham Wolds he had tried hard to curb the outbursts which had punctuated and to a degree soured, his dealings with the Operations Staff at Waltham Grange. At Ansham Wolds - once the irretrievably dead wood had been culled - he was at pains to give everybody a fair crack of the whip. However, on days like this when he was driving his crews to the limits of their endurance the sensibilities of the Ops Staff came very, very low down his list of priorities.

The briefers would buck up their ideas or heads would roll.

Chapter 5

Monday 3rd January, 1944
The Gatekeeper's Lodge, Ansham Wolds, Lincolnshire

The snow had stopped falling by the time Adam brought the Bentley to a skidding, sliding halt outside the cottage. He switched off the headlamps, sat for a moment in the frigid, pitch darkness. Briefly, he shut his eyes.

Images of the previous night's debacle came flooding back. A film of silvery cloud had covered Berlin. Hundreds of searchlights had played across the cloud floor as the battered remnants of the Lancaster Force droned slowly over the city. Line upon line of fighter flares hung in the sky, stacked in serried ranks. Heavies fell trailing plumes of flame. Isolated groups of Sky Markers drifted down far, far away while the flak rose in tight, radar-predicted boxes. Exhaustion, storms and an eighty mile-an-hour crosswind had scattered the bomber stream and the fighters and the gunners had tormented the survivors over Berlin.

R-Robert had rocked and jolted through the flak.

'Bomb bay doors open!'

Round Again had spotted a promising cluster of Sky Markers, asked permission to bomb them with his customary solemnity. Adam had checked with Ben if he had any idea which area of the city they were flying over.

'Tegel? Wittenau? God knows?' The navigator had responded, irritably. 'Take your pick, Skipper.' Ben had been in no mood to conceal his frustration. R-Robert's *H2S* set had burst into flames over Texel, ten-tenths cloud all the way from the Zuider Zee to the target had frustrated every attempt to get a ground fix since and towering electrical storms over Saxony had made it impossible to obtain accurate star sights. 'Somewhere over Berlin, anyway!'

'I could have told you that, old man!' Adam drawled, acidly. 'Are you listening to this, Round Again?'

'Bomb-aimer to pilot. Yes, Skipper.'

'We'll unload on your Sky Markers. Over!'

R-Robert had bombed somewhere in the Berlin area at 02:51 that morning and landed back at Ansham Wolds at 06:32 after a mercifully uneventful, unmolested return flight over storm-tossed northern Germany. By then another 27 Lancasters had been sacrificed on the increasingly blood-soaked altar of the main aim.

Adam had not slept. Until last night 647 Squadron had gone four operations without losing an aircraft: now B-Beer, M-Mother and S-Sugar were missing. B-Beer with a crew of sprogs; M-Mother manned by a scratch crew of old hands, including the squadron's Bombing and Gunnery Leaders; and S-Sugar with a veteran all-sergeant crew on its twenty-sixth op.

He badly needed to sleep.

Group Captain Alexander had been rushed to hospital in Hull that afternoon; the Padre had gone with him. The Old Man was in a bad way, having slid downhill while his heavies were away. They said he might not see out the night.

Adam wished he could remember the faces of B-Beer's sprogs. He shook his aching head and opened his eyes. It was no good moping over these things. No good at all. Pushing open the door he clambered out of the Bentley, trudged up to the door of the Gatekeeper's Lodge. The door opened before he could knock.

Eleanor, candle in hand, smiled.

"I'm sorry," he shrugged. "I haven't woken you up, have I?"

"It is quite late," she replied, bright-eyed. Her hair was dishevelled, she held a shawl and a woollen robe close about her shoulders over a pale cotton ankle-length nightdress. "Come inside, darling. Before you let the cold in."

He followed her into the cottage, the door shut behind him.

"I'm sorry, I didn't think," he said, feeling like an oaf. "I just wanted to see you. I didn't think. It's late. I should go..."

Eleanor viewed him forbearingly, patiently, fondly in the flickering candlelight. Carefully, she put the candle down on the sideboard in the narrow hallway. She stepped up to him, stretched her arms around his neck, and with a sigh, sank into his embrace.

He planted a kiss in her tousled hair and she looked up.

"You're tired," Eleanor murmured.

"You, too."

"A little. Adelaide's not very well and I didn't get back from the Rectory until late. And Emmy's sickening for something. I hope it's not this flu that's been going around," she explained. "I'd just dropped off to sleep when I heard the car in the lane."

"I'm sorry."

"Don't be, darling," she chided him, shivering involuntarily. "Let's sit by the fire."

Adam followed her into the parlour, peeling off his greatcoat. The embers of the fire were warm enough to chase away the worst of the cold. Eleanor settled herself on his lap, cuddled close.

"I've told you about my day," she whispered. "Now you must tell me about your day, darling."

Her nearness worked its magic on him. Despite himself, he chuckled.

"Nothing much to tell. Just another middlingly awful day, I suppose."

Eleanor rested her head on his chest, did not dare to meet his eye.

"How so, darling?"

"We lost three kites last night."

"Oh..."

"And the Station Master's been taken ill. Pneumonia. They've taken him to a Civvy hospital in Hull. It doesn't look good. He's in a bad way. A very bad way. Pro tem I'll be stepping into his shoes, I've already pretty much handed the Squadron over to Bob Nicholson."

Eleanor's heart leapt a beat. Unconsciously, she fingered the faded braid on his left breast, her thoughts in turmoil.

"Does that mean you won't be flying any more ops, darling?" She heard herself ask in a voice that might have belonged to a stranger.

"That's about the size of it," he admitted. "They'll wait and see if the Groupie will be fit to return to duty in the near future. That's not likely, but anyway, they'll wait and see, for a few days, then they'll look to install a safe pair of hands. Probably, sooner rather than later. Whoever it is, it won't be me. I'm due for a rest. So, no, the way things are, it's not likely I'll be flying any more ops. Not for a while."

Eleanor said nothing. There were no words. Her tiredness had flown out of the window. Adam yawned, held her tight.

"What's the matter?" He asked, placing a hand under her chin, gently raising her face. Her eyes were moist, full of tears. The woman sniffed, blinked at him, struggled free and got to her feet. She blew her nose, wiped away her tears, pushed the tangle of dark hair out of her eyes. The man levered himself out of the chair, took her by the shoulders. "What is it?"

Eleanor shook her head.

"I must look a terrible mess," she replied, avoiding his gaze.

He grinned, viewed her wryly.

"No. You're beautiful. Utterly beautiful..."

"No I'm not."

"Look me in the eye and say that!" He drew her closer, nuzzled her forehead, breathed in the musky scent of her.

Slowly, hesitantly, she tilted her head and in the soft, sepia light of the single candle her wet, sparkling brown eyes met his. She rested her arms on his chest, coaxed his mouth down to hers, met his parted lips with her own, melted against him.

They clung together, breathless, careless, all reserve discarded for the first time. Eleanor's robe fell open, the shawl slipped off her shoulders. His hands stroked the warm curves of her hips, reached about her waist, began to gather up the cotton of her nightdress. She giggled, started to squirm out of her robe, and undo the top buttons of his tunic. Kissing all the while, they danced together in the darkness by the glow of the flickering candle. Eleanor's robe fell to the floor, his hands stroked her curves through her thin cotton nightdress, her fingers explored his chest beneath the coarse serge of his battledress as she swayed softly, slowly in his arms.

They did not hear the girl tip toe downstairs, nor were they immediately aware of her presence as she stood watching them from the foot of the stairs with wide, curious eyes. Until, that was, she spoke.

"Mummy!" Emily said, timidly. Adam and Eleanor froze. "Mummy, I feel sick."

Chapter 6

Thursday 6th January, 1944
No. 1 Group Headquarters, Bawtry Hall, South Yorkshire

Adam swung the Bentley off the Doncaster Road, halted at the barrier. The sentry marched to the car, boots kicking up the snow and bent down to peer into the driver's window.

"Good morning, sir," he intoned. Adam flashed his pass. "Thank you, sir!" The guard straightened, saluted. The red and white pole lifted and Adam sent the car rolling up the freshly re-surfaced road to Bawtry Hall.

He nudged his passenger.

Squadron Leader Bob Nicholson stirred, groaned. "Are we there?"

"Afraid so, old man."

Nicholson groaned again, yawned, and stretched gingerly in the confines of the Bentley's cramped cockpit. He had got back late from Stettin that morning and had not slept.

"It's beyond me why the dates for these conferences have to be set in stone, sir," he complained, mildly.

Adam was warming to his second-in-command. He was a man who improved with acquaintance. Against expectations Bob was trying might and main to become a Lancaster man and to lead from the front. Last night O-Orange's port-inner had misfired just before the off; Bob had promptly commandeered the spare kite, L-Lincoln, getting away half-an-hour late. It was the sort of thing that impressed the crews and won over the waverers. The sort of thing that even impressed Adam Chantrey.

Nicholson glanced around at the snow-covered landscape. Ansham Wolds had escaped the fresh overnight snowfall. The worst falls were over the Pennines, in the west and north, thankfully, nowhere near most of the Lincolnshire and East Anglian bases of the Lancaster Force.

"I hope the AOC keeps it short and sweet today," Adam remarked. He wanted to get back to Ansham Wolds in time to drive the Rector up to Hull to visit Group Captain Alexander. A call to the hospital before setting off had confirmed that against all expectations the Groupie was still 'holding his own' and that a short visit would be in order.

"There's a first time for everything, sir," Nicholson replied, almost relaxing.

"We'll find out soon enough."

At the reception desk there was a message waiting for the 'OC, Ansham Wolds'.

"Would you report to Air Commodore Crowe-Martin please, sir?" the WAAF requested. "At your earliest convenience, sir."

Adam turned to Nicholson.

"I'll catch up with you later then, Bob. In the Mess, perhaps."

In the ante room outside the Deputy AOC's office, Adam was invited to take a seat. He preferred to stand and went over to the window to gaze out across the snow-covered building site. Figures tramped through the snow in the near distance, tractors rumbled over the frozen ground, a small crane swung over newly excavated foundations. The expansion went on apace, oddly disconnected from the war being fought over Germany.

Was it only seven weeks since the Chief had set the Lancaster Force on its collision course with the Big City? Seven weeks, a lifetime ago. Seven weeks and seventeen major attacks, ten of them on Berlin: over 400 heavies lost, including 300 hundred Lancasters; missing, down in the sea, crashed and written off in England. Seven grim weeks in which the whole pattern of the bombing war had changed; Lancasters to Berlin, Halifaxes to the other towns unless conditions were unusually propitious. Thus far the Halifax Force had sat out all bar two of the ten trips to the Big City.

Workmen in the snow hooked up a huge bucket to the jib of the crane. The crane's engine roared, coughed smoke, the bucket lifted into the air, moving clockwise, with a foreman walking ahead of it, waving and gesticulating at the crane operator.

The main battle would be over long before the current building work was completed, won or lost in the coming weeks by the men and the squadrons the Chief had to hand, now. Unless the Germans could be brought to their knees in the next month the great prize, the accomplishment of the main aim, would slip through the Chief's hands. Possibly, forever.

"Ah, Chantrey!" Called Air Commodore Crowe-Martin, bustling out of his office. "Come in, please."

Adam saluted, and followed the other man into his den.

"Alex is having a poor time of it, I gather," declared the Deputy Group Commander, waving the younger man to pull up a hard-backed chair. He made himself comfortable behind his big mahogany desk, fixing Adam in his flinty, grey stare.

"Yes, sir."

Crowe-Martin paused, sat back, framed against the high, arched windows.

"I hear that congratulations are in order on the matrimonial front?"

"Er, yes, sir," Adam muttered. "Thank you, sir."

"You're a damned lucky fellow!"

"Yes, sir."

The older man viewed him thoughtfully for a moment.

"Professor Merry always spoke very highly of you, you know," he said, lowering his voice, as if he was betraying a confidence. "Very highly."

Adam did not reply.

"Anyway," Crowe-Martin went on, smiling thinly. "In the circumstances, wherever he is now, the Prof would never forgive me if I let you go on flying ops a day longer than is absolutely necessary. So I'm not going to. The AOC plans to install a new Station Master at Ansham Wolds soonest. Bob Nicholson will *formally* take command of 647 Squadron on the twenty-first. That should give you time to do an orderly handover and for the new Station Master to get his bearings. It goes without saying that you're grounded pending posting."

"I see, sir." In a funny sort of way it was nice to have things spelled out.

"Screened," emphasised the Deputy Group Commander, adopting a somewhat schoolmasterish tone.

"Screened," Adam confirmed, blankly. "May I ask who the new Station Commander will be, sir?"

"No. You may not!" The older man's initial severity immediately thawed. He smiled. "You'll find out in good time. The AOC has asked me, in the absence of a senior officer at Ansham Wolds, to ensure that you keep both feet firmly on the ground until you leave 647 Squadron. In this connection he has asked me to ascertain why you felt it necessary to fly that last Berlin op?"

"Given the circumstances, I felt it was one of those nights when a CO was duty bound to set an example, sir."

Air Commodore Crowe-Martin frowned.

"Did you?"

"Yes, sir."

"Nevertheless, I won't have you doing it again. So, no more ops. Understood?"

"Yes, sir."

"And I'd be obliged to have your word on it."

Adam met the other man's eye.

"Of course, sir. You have my word on it."

There were no real surprises at the fortnightly conference. Nobody had expected the AOC to be complacent about the faltering progress of the campaign, nor to be overly sanguine about the apparent decline in the bombing performance of his squadrons since the opening blows of the battle. Henceforward, on some nights the Group's Lancasters would be required to operate at take off weights of up to 68,000 pounds. His audience accepted this edict in stoic silence. Most, like Adam, had seen it coming and had had their crews - or at least their old lags - flying training exercises at weights close to the new limit.

Adam and his passenger said very little on the journey back. Bob Nicholson dozed while his driver mulled over the dilemmas facing the Group Commander. Increasing the take off weights of the Group's heavies was no more than a gesture, an attempt to address the second of the three big problems facing the Main Force: target marking, bombing and morale, the unholy trinity of the war with the cities.

Marking, bombing and morale.

Marking: or more specifically, the fallibility of the Pathfinder Force. Given the fact that many Pathfinder squadrons had been virtually wiped out since November, it was hardly surprising that 8 Group's performance was *patchy*. The obvious solution was to rob the Main Force of its old lags, but that went against the grain. Half-hearted steps had been taken to facilitate the transfer of suitable crews from the Main Force Groups to the Pathfinders, but the Chief had set his face against widespread compulsion, perhaps because he, more than any man understood that it would be the last throw of the gambler's dice.

Bombing: Berlin, by dint of its sheer size, its broad streets, modern, well-founded buildings, open spaces, lakes, rivers and sandy soil was a remarkably tough nut to crack. The topography of the city demanded the heaviest possible bomb lift at the very moment the vulnerability – both in terms of performance and mechanical reliability - of the Halifaxes had resulted in their *de facto* withdrawal from the attack on the Big City. Arbitrarily raising the take off weights of the Group's Lancasters, in essence enabling each aircraft to carry a few extra cans of incendiaries, was not about to make good that deficit. However, given that the alternative was the piecemeal destruction of the Halifax Force it was inevitable that the Lancaster Force was destined to plough an ever bloodier furrow to Berlin, alone.

Morale: the great intangible. The crews were tired, fed up with being sent back time and again to the same, nightmarish target. Some crews - a tiny minority – were taking matters into their own hands to redress the odds by jettisoning their cookies over the North Sea. In the circumstances it was actually a minor miracle that so few crews had adopted this practice. Despite everything, the majority of crews continued to press on. Nevertheless, Adam recognised the deep weariness in the faces of his crews for what it was; a warning sign, one that Command ignored at its peril. Although his crews had operated on only twelve of the last fifty nights, they had been warned for ops on almost as many again, and spent days on end preparing for ops that were later cancelled. Moreover, Berlin was no three or four hour return hop to the Ruhr, every raid was a seven to ten hour ordeal that left a man physically and mentally drained for days afterwards. 647 Squadron had lost 13 aircraft in operations against the Big City since November; 9 missing, and 4 in crashes in England. Several neighbouring squadrons had fared worse, much worse. Half the crews who had flown in the first two attacks of the campaign were dead and this in just seven weeks. It was plain to see that the intensity of the battle was steadily, surely, fatally eroding the operational effectiveness of the squadrons, and grinding down the crews.

There were no easy answers, no bloodless solutions. The Pathfinders' problems were deep-rooted, probably irresolvable in the short term. Unless the Chief was prepared to sign the execution warrant of the Halifax Force, there was little that could be done to significantly increase the bomb lift to Berlin. And while the forthcoming Moon period might allow exhausted crews a few days respite it was little more than a stay of execution.

It was pitch black by the time the Bentley swung through the gates of RAF Ansham Wolds.

Adam went to his office. There were no letters to sign tonight, all of 647 Squadron's aircraft had returned safely from Stettin. Nor were there any notes or urgent files awaiting his return. He stalked down the corridor to look in on the Adjutant.

Tom Villiers was ensconced in his cubbyhole, angle-poise lamp pulled down over his blotter, immersed in a sheaf of papers. Rufus was curled up in his big, battered basket beside the desk. The Alsatian was the Adjutant's constant companion in the frequent absences of his master. Rufus got up and bounded over to welcome Adam, and they wrestled playfully for some moments.

"Anything I need to know about, Tom?"

"Nothing that won't wait until the morning, sir," replied the older man. "Any news from Group?"

Adam fought off Rufus and dropped into a chair. He dug out a cigarette and lit up. The big black German Shepherd sat in front of him, ears pricked, eyes excited, tail wagging. The Adjutant had recently taken steps to discourage the chaps standing the dog half-pints of stout, and issued strict and very specific instructions about what kitchen scraps Rufus was, and was not, to be given. Consequently, Rufus was already livelier and an altogether happier, trimmer beast than he had been for some months.

"No, nothing that won't wait until the morning." Adam liked the Adjutant. More important, he trusted him implicitly. Tom Villiers was a quiet, businesslike, reassuring tower of strength. Every inch the methodical, amiable country solicitor he had been before the war.

"Well said, sir," chortled the older man.

"The new Station Master is due down sometime next week," Adam confided, lowly. "Don't know who, yet. Group are keen that there should be an orderly handover period. I keep telling people that you're the chap they ought to talk to about that, but you know what the top brass are like. Never listen to a word a fellow says!"

Tom Villiers picked up his pipe.

"Do you know what the future holds for you, sir?" He inquired, packing the bowl, viewing the younger man over the top of his steel-rimmed spectacles. "Apart from wedded bliss, that is?"

Adam laughed.

"Wedded bliss," he echoed. "Yes, wedded bliss. Then I suppose it's a case of waiting and seeing."

The Adjutant struck a match, sucked on the stem of his pipe, disappeared behind a cloud of pungent, blue smoke.

"I shall miss Rufus," he declared, contemplatively, emerging from the fug. "I've a brace of retrievers at home. A place doesn't seem like home without a dog or two in it. I rang the hospital in Hull this evening, by the way. The Group Captain is still holding his own. I should think the Old Man's feeling rotten about leaving the station this way."

"Yes," Adam sighed. "I'd hoped to get over to see him today. I'll see if I can get away tomorrow. I promised I'd take the Rector up to Hull when I go. He'll be wondering what's happened to me."

Returning to his quarters Adam peeled off his jacket, splashed cold water in his face, combed his black, unruly hair. Crawford had laid out a change of uniform on his cot. He changed his shirt, pulled on his battledress tunic, hastily knotted his tie, scooped up his cap and headed out.

At the door something made him hesitate. He reached inside his tunic and took out his silver cigarette case; Helen Fulshawe's cigarette case. He stared at it for several seconds, and then, very deliberately, placed it on the table.

Chapter 7

Thursday 6th January, 1944
The Rectory, Ansham Wolds, Lincolnshire

Eleanor opened the door as Adam climbed out of the car. She stood framed in the light of the doorway, waved. He waved back and hurried up the path. They hugged briefly, kissed, went inside.

"Simon's been in bed all day," she explained, going ahead of him into the house. "The silly man went down to Kingston Magna yesterday to visit the Medwins. They've just had bad news from Italy. Their eldest boy. If I'd known Simon was going out I'd have tried to talk him out of it. You'd have thought he'd have known better after what's happened to poor Group Captain Alexander."

Johnny and Emmy jumped up when they heard voices and came to investigate. Adam ruffled the boy's hair, swept up the girl in his arms. Eleanor stepped back, watched him with the children. It struck her then, for the first time, how at ease he was with Johnny and Emmy, how natural it seemed for him to ruffle her son's fair hair, pick up Emmy. Her daughter giggled and squealed as he gently swung her to and fro.

"Have we been good today?" Adam asked, presently. Emmy nodded, fingering the lapel and the braid of his battledress. Johnny however, looked away, guiltily. It was then that the man noted the boy's grazed knees, and looked again at the scratch on his chin.

"Jonathan had a set to with Dennis, one of the

Bowman's evacuees," Eleanor reported, disapprovingly.

"He started it!" Johnny protested. "He pushed me off the wall."

"Oh, I see," Adam murmured.

"I had to pull them apart," Eleanor put in. "It's ridiculous. Most of the time they get on famously. But every now and then they fall out."

Adam put Emily down, settled on his haunches and looked Eleanor's son in the eye. "I thought Dennis was your best friend?"

"Yes."

"If I were you I'd make it up with him tomorrow."

"He pushed me off the wall!"

"Jonathan put a snowball down his neck," Eleanor interjected, wryly. Her son threw her a sulky look.

"Why, Wing-Commander!" Called Adelaide Naismith-Parry, hobbling into the room. "How lovely to see you, again."

Adam got up.

"Hello. I've just been hearing about Johnny's fisticuffs."

The Rector's wife beamed.

"That's a Grafton trait," she declared. "His grandfather was a stubborn fellow, you know. 'Never say die! Never a backward step!' That was his motto. I'm sure that's where young Johnny gets it from."

Eleanor blushed, turned away. Adam stepped into the breach.

"I popped in to apologise to the Rector. I mentioned I might be driving up to Hull to visit

Group Captain Alexander and had offered to take him with me. But if he's unwell..."

"How is dear Alex?"

"Bearing up, I gather. The worst may be over."

"Thank goodness."

Eleanor excused herself and disappeared into the kitchen. It was some minutes before Adam escaped and was able to join her. The woman smiled at him as he nudged the door shut at his back. Adelaide Naismith-Parry was talking loudly to the children, her voice sounded shrill even at a distance.

"I read the note you left for me at the Gatekeeper's Lodge," he explained.

"I've brought a pot of stew over," Eleanor explained, arranging pans on the stove. "Adelaide's inclined to flap when Simon's under the weather. I thought we might all have supper here. That way, I can make sure Simon's comfortable for the night." She spoke quickly, almost as if she was embarrassed, uncomfortable in his presence.

Adam understood her awkwardness and tried to allay her unease. When Emily had caught them in their passionate clinch on Monday night they had laughed and parted, feeling a little foolish. Circumstances had kept him away since then and they had had three days to think about what might have been.

"How is the Rector?"

"I think it is just a chill," she told him, not hiding her exasperation. "He was feverish yesterday evening when he got back from Kingston Magna. This morning the fever had broken. You wouldn't believe the trouble I've had making him stay in bed!"

Adam went up to her at the stove, circled her waist with his arms, drew her close, kissed the nape of her neck. Eleanor turned around in his arms, briefly covered his lips with her own, then held him away at arm's length.

"Emmy seems quite recovered?" He remarked mischievously.

"Yes. She was fine again in the morning." There was laughter in their eyes. "It's not funny, darling," Eleanor protested, giggling like a girl. "You really ought to go up and see Simon. He'd love to see you and as long as you stay in the kitchen, I'm not going to get a single thing done!"

Adelaide Naismith-Parry took the man upstairs.

"Simon, look who has come to see you!" The Rector was propped up in bed reading a dog-eared detective novel. He smiled broadly and immediately started to apologise for not being able to welcome his guest 'in a proper fashion'.

"I'm completely in the hands of the monstrous regiment of women," he complained, tongue-in-cheek. "Actually," he added, seeing his wife edging out of the room, "I don't know what I'd do without them!"

"Eleanor says you're on the mend, sir?" Adam began, perching at the bottom of the bed. "We need you to be on your best form for the wedding." The Rector tired swiftly. He spoke of his visit to Kingston Magna the previous morning, and inquired after Group Captain Alexander. He remarked in passing that to date, the winter was one of the worst he could recall. Adam left him dozing, arriving downstairs to find Eleanor laying the table.

"I went down to Group today," he said, without preamble. He leaned against the door frame. "The Deputy AOC called me into his room. You know, for a Head of House to junior prefect sort of chat. It's official, now. I'm grounded pending posting."

The woman's heart leapt, she carried on arranging the cutlery.

"I'm glad," she said, not trusting herself to look up.

"I'm due a fair bit of leave. I know we haven't discussed these things in any detail. Well, hardly at all, really. My fault entirely. Anyway, it would do us the world of good to get away from here for a spell. If you're amenable, we could honeymoon in the West Country, perhaps Cornwall. Tavistock, look in on my sister Hen. What do you think?"

Eleanor looked up.

"I think that's a lovely idea, darling."

Chapter 8

Thursday 6th January, 1944
RAF Ansham Wolds, Lincolnshire

Last night the fighters had gone to defend the Big City and the Lancaster Force had burned the heart out of Stettin.

Peter Tilliard sat back and groaned. His desk in C Flight's office at the southern end of No. 2 Hangar was no less cluttered than it had been that morning. Personnel files, action reports, maintenance updates, serviceability schedules, flying and training rosters sat in malignant, threatening heaps about him, each vying for his attention. He was dog tired yet restless, uneasy. There was a knock at the door. The door was open, the way he liked it to be.

George Simpson, his W/T operator peered into the gloomy office, a steaming mug in one hand, his cap in the other.

"ACW Croft said for me to bring you a cuppa char, Skipper," he grimaced, hesitating just outside the office.

Tilliard grunted.

"Bring it in then, George."

The sergeant W/T operator did as he was bade.

"Which one's ACW Croft?" Tilliard inquired, idly.

"The red head in the Squadron Office, Skipper."

"Oh, right." He remembered, now. ACW Croft was the dumpy girl with the nice eyes who worked for the Adjutant. She had been engaged to Barney

Knight's navigator, a bluff, hard-eyed fellow. Some afternoons she walked the Wingco's dog out by the far dispersals, cutting a sad, solitary figure dwarfed by the dark, brooding silhouettes of the heavies.

Simpson hovered, uncertain whether to stand his ground or run away.

Tilliard knew what was bothering his W/T operator. If George had the stomach for it this was probably as good a time as any to clear the air.

"Don't just stand there. If you've got something to say, spit it out, man!"

"Er, yes, sir."

Tilliard wrapped his hands around the mug of tea, raised it to his lips, sipped the brew and waited for Simpson to get his act together. So George wanted a 'sir' interview, did he?

"You know, sir, don't you?"

"If you say so, George."

"About my, er, sick record, sir?"

Tilliard nodded.

"What of it?" He asked it with an abruptness that struck Simpson like a slap in the face. The W/T operator stiffened, swallowed hard, and forced himself to continue.

"I was worried you might think I was, er, a..."

"Fringe merchant?"

"Yes, sir."

Tilliard looked him straight in the eye.

"Are you?"

Simpson returned his stare.

"No, sir!"

"That's all right then. And cut out this 'sir' nonsense, dammit!"

"Yes, sir. I mean, Skipper."

Tilliard put down the mug, rose to his feet, stretched and gazed through the grimy window into the heart of the giant hangar. Under the dazzling arc lamps erks were clambering over one of his Lancasters. The erks never stopped working on their charges, coming and going in anonymous relays.

"If I'd known you'd been dodging ops I'd never have had you in the crew, George. I'd have thrown the book at you. I don't care why you did it, although I can guess. Take my word for it, your feet wouldn't have touched the ground, you'd have been off the Squadron." He turned around, looked the other man in the eye. "But that was then. Now you're a member of *my* crew. The chaps have accepted you, you're good at your job and from what I've seen as steady under fire as any of us. So, so far as I'm concerned the slate is wiped clean. Blot your copybook again and I'll come down on you like a ton of bricks. But otherwise, I don't give a damn about anything that happened before you flew with me. Clear?"

Simpson gathered himself.

"Yes, Skipper!"

The W/T operator almost ran out of the office.

Tilliard dropped into his chair, stared through the window at the erks toiling over the big, black bombers in the body of the hangar.

"Can I file any of these for you, sir?" Asked LAC Tait, his bleary-eyed Flight Clerk, indicating the papers heaped on the desk.

"No. Leave them, please. I'm going for a walk. I need to blow away a few cobwebs."

It was bitterly cold outside the hangar and the

wind whipped across the fields, stinging exposed flesh, watering Tilliard's eyes. He made for his quarters where he found Jack Gordon sound asleep, snoring loudly. Having paid his intended, the fair Nancy a visit that afternoon, Jack had rolled back up the hill at dusk seven sheets to the wind. Happily sozzled he had gone straight to bed.

There were few revellers in the Mess, everybody was too tired. Although the previous night's attack on Stettin had turned out to be a quiet trip all round, it had been a very, very long haul.

His letter to Suzy still sat where he had left it, on the table by his cot, folded neatly in its unsealed envelope. Tilliard had written it a day ago while he waited for the off to Stettin, planning to post it that morning. Something had stopped him sealing the envelope and sending it on its way.

Jack stirred, rolled onto his back, snored once more and slept on. Thankfully Jack had got over his bad patch, battled through to the other side and rediscovered his sense of humour.

Peter Tilliard sat on his cot and steeled himself to reread the letter.

Dear Suzy,

I'm truly sorry things have come to this. But things are what they are and there is not a lot you or I can do about it. I daresay there's nothing to be gained by moping over it.

I'd hoped coming down to Waltham Grange would settle things, that we'd pick up where we left off before you went to Shrewsbury. It was not to be. Perhaps, I've changed. Perhaps, we've both changed. Who knows? I thought it might just be me, but then you've not been in touch since we said goodbye at Waltham Grange, so I've rather taken it as read that things are the same for you. I'm sorry it has turned out this way. I am immensely fond of you and I always will be. How could I not be? The trouble is I don't think I'm the fellow you knew in the beginning.

Oh dear, I'm not saying this very well. I feel such a cad, as if I've treated you abominably. If I have, I'm sorry with all my heart. The thing is I can't go on with this. It is wrong. It was one thing when I truly believed that whatever happened I was going to come through in one piece. But I no longer believe I will come through. I'm not sure when I stopped believing it, but the fact is I don't think I will survive. Too many fine chaps have gone for a burton since I've been here. Hardly anybody completes a tour these days.

So, I think it's for the best if we end it now. If we go on it will only end badly. Not for me, but for you and I think I have hurt you enough already.

Finishing now is for the best.
I am sorry. Please forgive me.
Yours,
Peter

Tilliard thought about ACW Croft alone with her grief as she walked the far dispersals where the ghosts of countless aircrew roamed. Perhaps, as she walked between the silent Lancasters she was communing with those ghosts, attempting to make her peace with her dead sweetheart. His hands shook as he folded the letter and put it back in the Manila envelope. He licked the flap, sealed it. There were tears in his eyes and a great weight in his chest.

    The thing was to carry on.

    Nothing else mattered, now.

Chapter 9

Thursday 6th January, 1944
The Gatekeeper's Lodge, Ansham Wolds, Lincolnshire

A crescent moon had climbed high into the clear, starry sky by the time Adam drove Eleanor and the children down the hill. A hard, biting frost was spreading across the land. Inside the cottage the man set about stoking the fire in the parlour while Eleanor bustled Jonathan and Emily into their beds. The boy and the girl were tired, it was long past their normal bed time and tonight they went meekly to their beds.

Adam busied himself with the fire, listened to the children moving about upstairs and Eleanor's gentle, coaxing tones. Presently, the woman came down, yawned. She smiled sleepily, walked into his arms.

"How will we get down to Cornwall?" She asked, lifting her face.

"I'm sure somebody will lend us a car," he replied, shrugging. "The Bentley's fine, but we can't expect Johnny and Emmy to sit on the luggage, can we? Not all the way down to the West Country?"

"No," she murmured. When he had suggested going down to Cornwall she had worried about leaving the children behind; it had never occurred to her that Adam had assumed that the four of them would travel together as a family.

"I suppose not. You don't mind Emmy and

Johnny coming along on our honeymoon, then?"

"Mind?" He laughed. "Of course not. They'll love it down there. Besides, we should start the way we mean to go on, what?"

Eleanor laid her cheek against his chest.

"Now I feel a little guilty," she confessed.

"How so?"

"I didn't realise you'd thought things through." Once more, she looked up into his eyes. "I'm sorry, I should have known better, shouldn't I?"

Damp logs crackled and fizzed, spitting, flaring in the heart of the fire. The bright, roaring flames lit their faces, painted their features dull ochre, and flashed in their eyes. Eleanor took his hand, stepped back.

"Whatever shall I do with you?" He made no reply, gently squeezed her hand. She went up on tip toe, brushed his lips with hers. "Come to bed, darling," she whispered.

"What about Johnny and Emmy?" Adam asked, his voice suddenly hoarse, cracking, strangled. When, three evenings ago, Emily had interrupted them - if not actually in *flagrante delicto* then moments away from it - he had felt more than somewhat ridiculous, and perversely, a little relieved. Something happened to him when he was with Eleanor, close to her, within her thrall. He became a stranger to himself, lost in her. He ached for her, yearned to hold her in his arms, feel her flesh against his own, warm, soft and fragrant in the darkness. It was like a dream, a perfect, waking dream.

"They are tired out, darling," she smiled, leading him towards the stairs. "And we shall bolt the bedroom door."

He followed, sleepwalking under her spell. At the foot of the stairs he pulled himself together, encompassed her waist with his arm, drew her to him.

"I love you," he muttered in her ear.

Eleanor sighed, kissed his mouth wetly, slowly. The stairs creaked loudly, deafeningly in the stillness of the cottage. They crept guiltily past the children's room, and ghosted into the bedroom. Adam heard the bolt slide home. The moonlight filtered through the net curtains. As his eyes adjusted to the faint twilight he moved to draw the curtains but Eleanor touched his elbow in the gloom. He turned, looked to her in the moonlight.

"No," she mouthed, her eyes glistening pools in the loom of the rising Moon. "Leave them, darling. It's romantic. Make love to me in the moonlight. It's perfect."

Even in the coldest weather the bedrooms of the cottage were snug and warm. The building had thick flint walls, a heavy thatched roof and the wide, brick chimney around which it stood constantly warmed the inner walls of the bedrooms. Tonight, despite the frost settling hard on the ground across Lincolnshire, inside the old cottage, a memory of warmth remained as if the Moon was a mystical faraway, second, cold sun.

In the bedroom Adam trembled as he bent his face to Eleanor's, covered her mouth with his. She wrapped her arms around his neck, clung to him. They kissed, tongues exploring, probing, licking. Unhurriedly, Eleanor began to unfasten the buttons of his battledress tunic as their lips touched, brushed one against the other. His hands stroked the curve of her hips, her thighs, the small of her back, caressing, fondling. He unbuckled the cotton belt gathering her dress at the waist. It fell at their feet. He wriggled out of his tunic. It too, fell at their feet as they kicked off their shoes. One of his shoes bounced away under the bed, clunking noisily as it came to rest up against the chamber pot. They both paused, tensing, listening briefly in the silence.

Eleanor giggled, blinked up at the man. Adam smiled, lifted his hands to her face, carefully brushed away the tangle of black hair from her eyes, and kissed her brow. He breathed her in, groaned with the joy of it. She giggled, again. Girlishly, mischievously, she took his hands and placed them on her breasts, briefly held them on her, pressing down. She shivered with pleasure, sighed, closed her eyes, swayed in the moonlight as she unbuttoned the man's shirt, ran her fingers over his ribs, over his bare skin while he fumbled clumsily with the clasps of her frock. Their movements were less measured, faster, less sure, now. The dress came off Eleanor's shoulders; her fingers groped at the waistband of Adam's trousers, stroked him as he hardened underneath. The dress crumpled around her hips. In an instant she had shrugged out of her lacy, white petticoat, it too rested in folds on her hips. Momentarily, Eleanor's partial nakedness in the moonlight paralysed the man, took his breath away. He stared at her, marvelled at the wildness of her hair, the exquisite pale beauty of her, felt humble, protective, utterly lost in lust for her, his thoughts in chaos and yet somehow, peaceful. He wanted to worship her, possess her; save her from all ill, despoil her, penetrate her, to be inside her forever. Eleanor stopped giggling, pulled the shirt off his back. With an aching, moaning inner release her dress and slip dropped to the floor, and Adam's trousers fell about his ankles. They stood naked, separate for an instant. Their eyes met.

"You're beautiful," he muttered. "So beautiful."

She lowered her eyes, her fingers traced patterns on his boyish, almost hairless chest.

"So are you, darling," she said, very huskily.

He knelt down, nuzzled her belly, planted a dozen reverent, tender kisses on her bare skin: first on the round of her abdomen, her navel, then on the points of her hips, and with immense deliberation, as if at prayer, in the warm blackness between her thighs. She ran her fingers through his tousled hair as he kissed her, drank in her essence, worshipped her. Eleanor half-turned, parted herself a little, leaned against the side of the bed as Adam rose to his feet. She reached for him, took him in her hand, held him, positioned herself on the bed and drew him onto and into her, deeply as his mouth found hers.

He lay inside her, on her for a long time. They remained very still, clinging together as they kissed in the shadows. All was quiet, in the cottage and outside. No wind stirred the barren branches of the trees in the woods, no sound of passing aircraft disturbed the sky. They were alone in the moonlight, their hearts beating close together, almost as one. Outside bleak midwinter held the countryside in its icy grip, while inside they were warm, safe from all evil. The woman moved her hips against him, settled and lay unmoving, content to have and to hold him within her. Her hands stroked his back. Adam propped himself up on his elbows, viewed her with a wonderstruck awe as if he could hardly believe what was happening.

"What?" She whispered, half-smiling.

"Nothing."

"Tell me?" Eleanor insisted, her brown eyes wide, bright and moist.

"Do you believe in love at first sight?"

"I think so."

Adam was drunk with her, his head reeling.

"I've loved you from the start," he confessed. "From the first time I laid eyes on you, my love."

Eleanor sniffed, said nothing. Tears tricked down her cheeks.

"Make love to me, darling," she sighed. "Make love to me."

He moved in her, rose and fell upon her. Slowly, slowly as the woman lay quiescent, moaning softly, softly with every thrust. The bed creaked, but quietly. The Moon shone in through the window bathing the lovers in its cold, silvery light. When at last the man was spent he rolled off her, and she nestled in the crook of his arm.

"Don't go," she pleaded. "Stay with me."

"I'm not going anywhere," he promised.

"Good." Eleanor laid her head on his chest, listened to his heartbeat. "That first day," she said, out of the blue. "When I recognised you on the platform. That was it for me, too, darling. Ever since then, you've well, been with me. You've been with me all the time. Every minute."

Hush descended between them.

"Look," the man said, eventually. "I don't know if it's talking out of turn. But just before he died the Prof asked me why I hadn't proposed to you. He came straight out with it. Bold as you like."

"Oh. What did you say, darling?"

"I told him it wouldn't be fair on you."

Eleanor giggled, pinched him playfully.

"Because of the Squadron, or because of Helen Fulshawe?"

"Both, I suppose."

"Silly man," the woman chided him. Their voices were low whispers, barely audible even though they were speaking almost into each other's ear. "I had several lovers before I married Harry."

"Oh?"

"Don't sound so surprised, darling"

"Sorry," he laughed ruefully.

"You're not jealous?" She asked, anxiously.

"Of course not."

Eleanor allowed herself a small sigh of relief.

"I was always faithful to Harry. Even when things started to go badly for us. Oh dear, can we talk about something else?"

Adam turned onto his side to face her in the moonlight.

"For what it's worth, the Prof told me that if we married we'd have his blessing."

Eleanor gazed at him wordlessly, lifted her mouth to his and kissed him.

"I wondered if he'd said anything," she said, breathlessly. She paused, caught her breath, and went on. "He told me about the letter you wrote to him when David was shot down. How it helped make things bearable. How it gave him hope. I know you two had your differences but he thought the world of you."

Adam did not trust himself to speak, instead he buried his face in Eleanor's hair, let the scent of it distract his senses and feed his longing.

"It must have been Simon who told you Father was ill?" Eleanor prompted. The question was put fondly, rhetorically. "And about that dreadful little Rowbotham man?"

"He was only thinking of you."

"I know."

The man put a finger to her lips.

"No more questions."

Eleanor gave vent to another giggle; a giggle that turned the man's loins to tingling liquid, sent a tremor of pure, wanton lust up his spine and rendered him incapable of coherent thought.

"I'm sorry. No more questions, Wing-Commander." She laughed as he rolled her onto her back, spread her legs wide. He mounted her, penetrated her, rocked back and forth on her, in her; she closed her eyes, joined her hands behind his back, rolled and pushed, writhed against him, moaning, whispering in his ear.

"I love you, love you, love you..."

They were lost one in the other, locked together.

A cloud passed across the crescent of the Moon as they fell together, exhausted. After the cloud had scudded aside a sheen of perspiration glinted dully on them, their chests heaved, they lay panting for breath, dazed, confused and a little shocked by the abandon of the act. When eventually Adam's pulse had steadied he leaned across, cupped Eleanor's left breast in his hand, lightly toyed with the erect nipple. She covered his hand with her own, clutched it tightly against her.

"Oh dear," she gasped. "If that doesn't wake up the children, nothing will."

Chapter 10

Friday 14th January, 1944
RAF Waltham Grange, Lincolnshire

The operations order spewed out of the teleprinter on an endless roll of paper at noon. The old Moon was on the wane, the weather had broken and the Lancaster Force was gathering itself to strike deep into the German hinterland.

388 Squadron had been called to readiness at nine that morning and Suzy had been in the Operations Room ever since. Across the airfield the crews were inspecting their aircraft, preparing to start flight testing within the next hour. The big Matador fuel bowsers were queuing in the drizzle to take on their loads of 2,500 gallons of 100-octane, the armourers were wheeling out trains of cookies and incendiaries. Down in the crowded Operations Room people spoke in whispers, phones rang, bodies jostled around the readiness boards, specialists clustered around charts and Acting-Squadron Leader Ramsey, the newly promoted Operations Officer pawed impatiently over the ops order.

"Where's it to be tonight?" Demanded the CO, Wing-Commander Clive Irving, striding into the bunker like Christ come to cleanse the Temple. "The bloody Big City, I suppose?"

Ramsey jumped, startled.

"Er, afraid not, sir," he replied, apologetically. "Brunswick, actually. Spoofs to Magdeburg and Berlin, a spot of *Gardening* over the Frisians, otherwise the normal drill, sir."

"Brunswick?" Irving retorted loudly, angrily twirling the right-hand bar of his moustache. Everybody in the room knew he was playing the moment for dramatic effect. It was all part of the game. "What in Hell's name is worth bombing in Brunswick?"

Suzy was standing behind the Operations Officer's shoulder. With a supreme effort of will she maintained a straight face. When she had arrived at Waltham Grange scarcely a month ago the atmosphere had been not unlike that at Ansham Wolds in the bad old days. Since then, Clive Irving had single-handedly grabbed the Squadron by the scruff of the neck, shaken it like a big dog with a juicy bone between its jaws, and turned its fortunes around by sheer force of personality. The CO's demeanour made no concessions to subtlety, not for him the meticulous attention to detail and the quietly terrifying, relentless efficiency of a man like Wing-Commander Chantrey. The CO reminded Suzy more of poor, mad Bert Fulshawe, albeit a younger, rather more handsome reincarnation. A much, much more handsome reincarnation who had somehow retained a fully functioning sense of humour. Clive Irving had imprinted his dashing, boisterous persona on 388 Squadron. Brash, Devil may care, utterly fearless he charged around Waltham Grange like a bull in a china shop.

"Messerschmitt factories, sir," Ramsey said, hesitantly, apologetically.

Irving grinned wolfishly, lit a cigarette.

"Bugger the Messerschmitt works," he declared,

sniffing. "Fighter factories are no use to me, old man! What about something that'll burn? What about some nice wooden houses? Lots and lots of them in good-old fashioned narrow streets?"

The Operations Officer's jaw hung loose for a moment. Suzy stared at her feet, suspecting the Wingco only said these things to shock, to keep them all on their toes.

"Let's not get squeamish, old man!" Irving barked at his Operations Officer. "We're all in the same game, here. What!"

"Yes, sir." Not for the first time in recent weeks Ramsey was visibly unnerved. "The er, AP, is, er, located slightly south of the *Altstadt*, I believe."

"Jolly good. Next to the *Altstadt*, eh. No shortage of kindling, then?"

"No, sir."

"Good show! Nothing like a good bonfire, that's what I say! What about the route. Straight in, again, I suppose?"

"Pretty much, sir. Texel to the line Hamburg - Hanover, then a south-south-east leg in to the target."

Irving paused, glanced up at the big map of Western Europe – an exact copy of the one in the Briefing Hall - on the far wall of the bunker. As yet nobody had put up the route-marker ribbons. He ran his eye along the proposed route. His half-smile became a scowl, the laughter in his eyes faded, to be replaced with a deadly seriousness.

"Right," he decided. "You can give me a full briefing at thirteen hundred hours. Flight commanders, Nav and Bombing Leaders, Intelligence and Met Officers to attend. We'll set the main crew briefing for sixteen hundred hours."

Irving stalked out.

The Operations Officer allowed himself a surreptitious sigh of relief, and wiped his brow. Then, realising everything had come to a halt he turned around, surveying the bunker.

"Well, you heard what the CO said! Let's get weaving!"

Suzy went back to her chair. The operations order, printed on a continuous roll, was being torn into sections. Presently, a sheaf of papers sat before her. Quickly, she sorted them and began to dictate to her WAAFs. Typewriters rattled. Copies of the relevant orders needed to be communicated to the appropriate section heads, instructions regarding fuel and bomb loads had to be sent out, everything had to be checked and double-checked, with as little as possible left to chance. The slightest inattention to detail, a momentary lapse on her part might, quite literally, be the death of somebody and whenever she started to flag, she constantly reminded herself of this fact. She was glad to be busy, if only because it took her mind off Peter Tilliard's unopened letter. He had not written to her until now and she knew in her heart what it must signify. She hoped she was wrong but knew she was not. She wished there was somebody she could talk to, a girl friend in the Waafery, but there was nobody. At Ansham Wolds she had struggled to make friends, likewise, here at Waltham Grange she had met no kindred spirit. Other of course, than Maggie Warren, who was gone. She would read Peter's letter, later.

Later.

Outside, the gates of the station had been locked. Phone lines had been physically disconnected at the station switchboard, and armed sentries posted at all key points as the airfield progressively built up to the off. The Lancasters would be test flown, bombed up and fuelled. Erks would clamber over the bombers, remedying any faults identified during the flight tests. The crews would go for a meal and begin the round of specialist briefings which culminated in the main crew briefing. Afterwards, they would dress for the off, and hang around waiting for the buses to take them out to the heavies.

Suzy looked up.

They were plotting the route on the big map on the wall. The red ribbons arrowed across Holland, into Germany near Meppen, due east passing below Vechta and on to Celle, where they dog-legged into the south towards Brunswick, some hundred miles short of Berlin. The crews hated these long, straight legs across northern Germany, regarding them – from painful past experience - as accidents waiting to happen.

'It makes it too bloody easy for the Jerries to work the route,' Clive Irving had remarked calmly, conversationally after the New Year's Day trip to the Big City. Slumped greyly, wearily at the debriefing table he had made no secret of his frustration. 'We're making life far too bloody easy for the Jerries!'

The imaginative route employed on last week's Stettin raid had given the crews hope that Command had woken up, belatedly, to the realities of the battle over Germany. Unfortunately, it seemed the lessons learned that night had already been discarded.

The crews would not be impressed.

Chapter 11

Friday 14th January, 1944
RAF Ansham Wolds, Lincolnshire

Adam leaned on the door of the Station Commander's car. Tom Villiers stood at his shoulder. The WAAF driver, a large, horsy girl stamped her feet in the cold as they watched the Anson trainer swoop out of the grey sky, bump and jolt along the runway, slow down, wheel to the left and taxi towards the hard stand. The wind plucked at their coats, its icy touch watering their eyes.

Even as the twin-engine trainer pulled off the main runway the next Lancaster, big, black and menacing drifted in over the threshold, flaps fully extended, Merlins desynchronized. It landed heavily. Tyres squealed painfully. The pitch of its Merlins fell as the pilot throttled back. In the distance, more aircraft joined the circuit, swinging ponderously across the sky, lining up with the runway like great prehistoric birds, dark and menacing against the low clouds.

The moment the Anson rumbled to a halt two erks rushed forward, kicked large, wooden chocks under its wheels. Another went to the fuselage door, pulled it open and clipped it back. Adam straightened, adjusted his battledress and strode towards the aircraft. The Adjutant followed two steps behind. It was not much of a welcoming party but the Wingco had forewarned him that the new Station Master was a man who would take a dim view of any 'distracting ceremonials' when the Squadron was in the middle of gearing up for a Goodwood.

Adam had taken the telephone call from Group twenty-four hours ago.

'Ah, Chantrey,' Air Commodore Crowe-Martin had prefaced, his tone stiffly formal. 'You'll be glad to hear that the AOC has appointed Group Captain Farlane to Ansham Wolds...' A kit bag tumbled out of the door of the Anson, then a big, battered wooden trunk appeared. Two erks wrestled this to the ground, snapping to attention at the first sight of the new Station Master in the door.

Pat Farlane stuck his head outside the fuselage.

He was grinning broadly.

Adam stepped up, grabbed his old friend's arm as he clumsily, awkwardly negotiated the rungs of the steps to the damp tarmac. Farlane breathed in the frigid Lincolnshire air and took his bearings.

The two men looked at each other.

There were no smiles, not for a moment. Both men could not help but be struck by the strange poignancy of this reunion. They were after all the last survivors of the Wilhelmshaven raid reunited in arms, the shield-bearers for the dead of that long ago December afternoon. They were old in the ways of the war, inured to its cruelties and its tragedies. They had lost so much, somehow survived until now to witness the final battle, to be witnesses at Armageddon. Neither man would have chosen any other fate. They were thinking the same thoughts, kindred souls honestly not knowing whether to laugh or cry. The cold stung

Adam's eyes, he blinked back tears. He remembered the Wilhelmshaven disaster and all the fine fellows who had died that day; remembered also visiting Pat in hospital in the days after he lost his leg.

'I'll be back, you'll see!' The older man had whispered, vehemently.

His friend had hung suspended between life and death for a week but Adam had always believed he would pull through. Known it intuitively. Just as he had always known that some day they would serve together again, and once more pick up the sword and drink to the dead of Faldwell, Kelmington, Waltham Grange, Ansham Wolds and the half-a-hundred other blood-soaked outposts of the Main Force.

Adam saluted crisply.

"Welcome back, sir."

Pat Farlane returned his salute, and replied with a gruff, forced severity.

"It's damned good to be back, Wing-Commander."

Tom Villiers watched from a respectful distance. It was one of those occasions when he - a deskbound warrior - felt wholly excluded from the brotherhood of the fighting men who rode Bomber Command's heavies to Germany. The Wingco and the new Groupie looked at each other for a moment, laughter in their eyes. Old friends reunited and vindicated. Old friends, survivors despite everything. Old friends thinking of comrades long gone. In the background a Lancaster taxied past, deafeningly, its pilot gunning his port outer Merlins, swinging the bomber onto its nearby hard stand.

"God, it's good to be back!" Pat Farlane announced, misty-eyed. "Damn it, it's good!" He stuck out his right hand, took Adam's hand in his own. "So damned good!"

To Tom Villiers' astonishment the two men suddenly abandoned all formality, and spontaneously embraced. For a moment he was afraid they were going to dance a jig. The Adjutant lowered his eyes in embarrassment, a little ashamed of himself. He was not alone in his discomfiture. Neither the watching erks, nor the WAAF driver knew what to do with themselves.

"God, Adam! You don't know how good it is to be back!" Pat Farlane repeated, enthusiastically slapping the younger man on the back. With a supreme effort of will he remembered himself, composed himself somewhat, casting an eye at the bombers orbiting the airfield. "Right. I take it we're on for tonight?"

"Goodwood to Brunswick, sir."

"Jolly good!"

Adam introduced the new Station Commander to the Adjutant: "Tom's the chap who actually runs this place, sir."

"Oh, I wouldn't say that, sir," Villiers protested.

"Good to meet you, Tom." Farlane sized him up and returned the Adjutant's salute. His scrutiny was searching without being unkind. "You and I will get together later. I shall rely on you to tell me what's what around these parts."

"Yes, sir."

Farlane turned back to Adam.

"Brunswick, eh? How many kites are we

putting up?"

"Twenty-four."

"Capital! Capital! How's poor old Alex, by the way?" He asked, slumping into the back seat of the staff car.

Adam had taken the Rector up to Hull to visit Group Captain Alexander in hospital the previous afternoon. Although his illness had taken a severe toll on him the Old Man had been much more his old self.

"On the mend, sir," he reported. "He's started worrying about being up and about in time for the wedding, actually."

"Good old Alex, you can't keep a good man down, what?"

"No," concurred the younger man. The Groupie was unlikely to return to active service. "He was in good form, yesterday. I finally got around to asking him how he got his MC. I never realised he flew Bristol Fighters in the first do."

Pat Farlane nodded.

"Quite a story, by all accounts. Boy's own stuff. I'll wager Alex didn't make anything of it. He wouldn't, of course."

"No, he was a bit vague. Said it was a lot of fuss about nothing and all that guff."

"That sounds just like Alex," Pat chuckled. "If I remember correctly, his Squadron got jumped by the Richthofen boys and he crashed in no-man's land. He broke his ankle, I think. When it got dark he crawled back to our side of the lines. The next morning the Jerries came swarming over the top. Alex being Alex persuades the brown types to splint him up, won't hear of being evacuated, grabs a rifle and takes his place in the line. When reinforcements finally arrived legend has it he was the last officer standing with dead Bosch all over the shop."

Adam stared out of the window as the car sedately traversed the aerodrome and his Lancasters swooped in to land, one after the other.

'Damned lungs,' Group Captain Alexander had remarked, philosophically. 'It's the cold that sets them off. Still, I've had a pretty good innings. All things considered. It doesn't do to mope about these things, what. So, I shan't. My wife has her heart set on a thatched cottage somewhere in the Home Counties. The least she deserves. We haven't stayed more than a year or two in one place in the last twenty. Palestine, India, Malta, Egypt, she's followed me all over, bless her. Oh, don't misunderstand me, my boy. We've had such great fun. Such a fine time. But I know she's always longed for a home. A proper home, as it were.'

"Take us to the Mess, please," Pat Farlane decreed.

"Yes, sir," acknowledged the WAAF driver.

Adam escorted the new Station Commander into the nearly deserted Officers' Mess. Farlane's keen eye swept the room, lingered momentarily on the profusion of marks - which could only have been footprints - on the ceiling above the bar.

"Ceiling walking and bicycle racing are standard drill here, sir," Adam told him, following his gaze.

Pat Farlane was impressed. The ceiling was a high one, a dozen feet if it was an inch. The chaps would need to form a seriously large pyramid of chairs, tables and bodies to raise a volunteer 'walker' into the approved 'walking' position. Adam called for a brace of pink gins and the two men settled by the fire.

"You've set a date for the wedding, I gather?"

"A fortnight tomorrow, all being well."

"You're a lucky blighter! But then you always did land on your feet, what?" A steward marched over, placed glasses on the table between the two officers. Pat Farlane signed the bar chit. "Absent friends," he proposed, lifting his glass,

"Absent friends," Adam echoed, aware of the older man's close scrutiny. Pat drew out a pack of cigarettes, American Lucky Stripes. They lit up, not speaking, both thoughtful, both mindful of the many pitfalls that as old confederates they owed it to each other to avoid.

"For the record," the older man said, lowly. "Bert Fulshawe was riding for a fall. The AOC knew it, I knew it and so did a lot of other chaps who ought to have known better. You mustn't blame yourself for what happened."

"Somebody marked Bert's card just before he bought it," Adam returned, in no mood to seek exoneration. The whys and wherefores were incidental. He felt responsible for Bert's death and that was that "Tipped him the wink about Helen. Blow by blow stuff, I gather."

Pat brushed this aside with a frown. Leaning forward he tapped Adam's knee, looked him straight in the eye.

"Adam, old son," he sighed, "for such a frightfully clever chap you can be awfully dense, sometimes! You are a clot, you know. What on earth makes you think that bloody letter put *you* in the frame?"

"I just assumed..."

"Look, old chap," Pat put in, tartly. "You've got every right to tell me I'm talking out of turn here, but it's not as if you're the only chap in Christendom who ever enjoyed Helen Fulshawe's, er, shall we say, favours."

Adam stared at him like an idiot.

Pat went on quickly.

"At least you were fairly discreet about it. You and Helen were one of the best kept secrets in Bomber Command, old chum!" Adam was dumbfounded. "Look," his old friend sighed, finding the conversation distasteful but determined to say what he had been meaning to say for some weeks. "Helen was involved with a Five Group type. Some fellow serving his time at Group before getting back onto ops. A couple of days before he was killed Bert went all the way down to Grantham to collar this chap in the Mess. There was a frightful scene. It was all hushed up of course, nobody wanted to make anything of it. So, when Bert had his, er, *accident*, the AOC took the opportunity to put the lid on it. I'm told Bert and this other chap had a real set to, they had to be pulled apart. The fact of the matter is that Bert should have been posted away from here when he was screened. That's what Alex wanted but the Wing-Commander (P) fouled up the paperwork. Bert wasn't like you and me, old son. Chaps like us walk away, live to fight another day. Not Bert. Nobody marked his card! Leastways, not the way you think. So forget it. Don't go blaming yourself."

Adam's guilt refused to be assuaged.

"Easier said than done," he said, doggedly.

"Please yourself, old son," Pat said, amiably. "Thought I'd fill you in, anyway." He drained his glass, sighed. "Now, let's get down to business."

"Yes, sir."

"Tell me what you know about Messingham Priory?"

Adam frowned.

"Not a lot, I'm afraid."

Bill Simmons and his crew were buried at Messingham. Bill, one of the four Boscombe Down 'musketeers': Porthos to Dave Merry's D'Artagnon.

"I hear the field's earmarked for a new OTU. Not due to open for a couple of months, yet. The place is still a construction site, isn't it?"

"Not for much longer."

"Oh?"

"Messingham Priory is to open a month ahead of schedule at the beginning of March as a satellite of Ansham Wolds under my command. Not as an OTU but as a fully-fledged Heavy Conversion Unit. If necessary, I'm to decommission one of 647's flights to provide an initial instructor cadre for the new unit."

Adam took this in, thought about it.

Pat sat back. "The AOC wants the first commander of 1671 HCU to be a 'real' ops man. A chap just like you, in fact."

"I see."

"No need to give me your answer now. Think about it. Sleep on it."

Chapter 12

Saturday 15th January, 1944
The Rectory, Ansham Wolds, Lincolnshire

Eleanor looked out of the kitchen window as a big, black, gleaming car stopped by the gate. The driver switched off the motor, jumped out and opened the passenger door. Out stepped a man in his thirties, a sturdy man with a ruddy complexion and a flowing handlebar moustache. A moustache suited some men better than others, Adam, bless him, would have looked ridiculous with such a moustache. But even from a distance she saw that it suited this man to a tee and it was then that she guessed who he was. When he walked around the car limping heavily, her guess was confirmed.

Group Captain Farlane paused to speak to his WAAF driver, turned and made his way stiffly, slowly up the path to the church. Eleanor watched him climb the hill and wend his way through the graves.

"A visitor?" Adelaide Naismith-Parry asked, peering at the staff car.

Eleanor started. She had not heard the Rector's wife hobble into the kitchen.

"I think it may be the new Station Commander but I don't think he's come to visit us. Not today."

"Oh, what a pity. Simon will be so upset to have missed him!"

"Never mind," Eleanor soothed, absently. The Rector had gone off in the car Adam had sent for him to Hull to pay another call on Group Captain

Alexander. "Will you be all right if I leave Johnny and Emmy with you for a few minutes, Adelaide?"

"Of course, dear."

"I'm just going to pop out for a moment." Gathering her coat Eleanor went out of the front door. "Excuse me," she mouthed, knocking at the window of the staff car to attract the driver's attention. The WAAF wound down the window and smiled. "Excuse me. Your passenger? Am I right in thinking it would be Group Captain Farlane?"

"Yes, Ma'am."

"Thank you." The churchyard steps were wet, slippery and the well-worn stones shone with the rain. Overhead the sky glowered and low clouds scudded above the Norman tower of the church. "Forgive me, Group Captain," she apologised, approaching the stranger.

Pat Farlane looked up. He had not heard her approach.

"Sorry, I was miles away," he murmured, distractedly. He had been in the middle, in fact, of telling Bert Fulshawe that all Groups had been warned for Frankfurt-am-Main that night. He had intimated to his old friend that there was a strong possibility the raid would be scratched because the weather forecast was irredeemably dire. Everybody was going through the motions but nobody actually believed the raid would go ahead. Normal drill. Bert knew the score. One old lag did not need to spell it out to another old lag.

"I'm sorry, I didn't mean to intrude."

"No, it's all right. Really. I was just saying hello to an old friend, that's all." It was said with utter sincerity. Bert Fulshawe's mortal remains might be buried in the ground at his feet but his spirit lived on. Old friends remained with a man forever.

Eleanor followed the movement of his eyes.

"I never really got to know Wing-Commander Fulshawe. The Rector and he were firm friends, but I only ever met him in passing. As one does."

The man smiled.

"As one does," he agreed. He held out his hand. "Farlane, Pat Farlane. And you must be Eleanor?"

They shook hands.

"I knew your father well," the man went on, viewing her indirectly. She was a dark, striking woman. She seemed a little tired and drawn but her brown eyes sparkled, radiated a profound inner strength. "I was dreadfully sorry to hear about his death. Very sorry. He was a good sort. I can't say the Prof and I always sang from the same song sheet, but you always knew with the Prof that his heart was in the right place and that he was on your side. Mind you, he could be an awkward so and so," he smiled, "but I shall miss him. We'll all miss him. Had it been possible I should very much have liked to come down for the funeral."

"I miss him very much." Eleanor said, simply. Pangs of loss, hurt beyond measure threatened to moisten her eyes, break her down. That would never do. "But we have to carry on, don't we? There's always so much to do. And I have Adam. He's been my strength these last few weeks."

"I gather the wedding's set for the twenty-ninth?"

"All things being equal."

Farlane laughed, gently.

"They will be if I have anything to do with it!"

They found themselves staring at the cross at the head of Bert Fulshawe's grave.

"Father's grave is over in the corner," Eleanor said. "At the end of the RAF plot. He didn't make any special requests but we thought it was appropriate. In the circumstances."

"Most appropriate. He's in good company." Farlane ran his eye down the line of graves, each with its clean white cross and meticulously maintained borders. He had learned from Tom Villiers that the graveyard was tended daily by defaulters from the station. It was one of a number of bridge-building 'local arrangements' Alexander had sanctioned shortly after Ansham Wolds opened. The Adjutant had asked him, very tactfully, if he wished to review these 'local arrangements'. 'Goodness, no!' He had quickly replied. 'Alex wouldn't have stood for anything irregular. Let things be, please.' Pat wondered what would happen to the graves when the war was over and the Lancasters were gone. Although, he had never subscribed to the view that the Main Force could bomb Germany out of the war by the spring, he firmly believed that the end was in sight. Then what would happen to the memories of the fallen?

"Of course, you'd have known Wing-Commander Fulshawe even longer than Adam?" Eleanor prompted.

"We passed out of Cranwell the same year." Farlane told her, stepping away from the grave. "Bert, Paul, Adam's older brother, and I. Bert and

Paul were as thick as thieves. Paul was a funny sort of chap. Full of himself, always liable to put people's back up but he'd never let you down in a tight spot. When your beloved first turned up at Faldwell Paul made Bert and me promise to keep an eye on him. 'Keep an eye on the snotty little sprog,' he said, 'one day he'll surprise us all!' I've always remembered that. Paul and Adam didn't really get on but I think in a funny sort of way Paul always understood Adam better than anybody. Paul would ring me or Bert every other day almost, checking to see how 'the snotty little sprog' was getting on. He was so proud when Adam qualified on Wellingtons. So proud, a bit choked, if you know what I mean?"

Eleanor risked a smile at this. They began to walk towards the path.

"You knew Paul was killed back in forty, I assume?"

She nodded.

"Those were good days, those pre-war days at Faldwell. Damned fine days," Pat recollected. "Then of course the war came and we all swanned off to Wilhelmshaven. After that everything changed. The old Squadron didn't exist anymore. That was the worst of it. The worst of times, as they say. Bert was in hospital for a while and I took over." A low, self-deprecating chuckle. "Until one night I landed a kite in Faldwell Fen, of course. Still, worse things happen at sea." Slowly, carefully they descended the path to the lane. "I must be off. An appointment at Group, I'm afraid," he explained, on nearing the car. "I am glad we've met at last."

"So am I. You must come round for tea one day."

"I'd like that."

Inside, Adelaide had turned on the radio and was listening to the light programme, awaiting the mid-day news when Eleanor returned.

"Group Captain Farlane was visiting the RAF plot in the churchyard," she informed the Rector's wife. "He was an old friend of Wing-Commander Fulshawe's. When he's settled in, I'm sure he'll call on Simon."

Eleanor took off her coat and went back into the kitchen. The children were playing in the woods below the Rectory and she paused to listen fondly to their voices. Moving to the sink she began to peel the potatoes for lunch. She put the kettle on the stove, humming softly, happily to herself. Sadness and joy, doubt and belief played on her, constantly. She had found and lost her father, stumbled into the arms of a man with whom she was hopelessly besotted and who miraculously, inexplicably, loved her also. The tides of the world were carrying her along, pulling her this way and that and she was powerless to resist or to chose any other course. And yet. And yet she was happy, blissfully content within herself.

The morning after they had made love she had woken in the twilight and instinctively reached out for Adam. Realizing she was alone in the bed she had awakened in a panic. But he had been there, bending over her, kissing her.

'I'm sorry, I didn't mean to wake you,' he had whispered in her ear. 'You looked so peaceful.

And so beautiful. It seemed wrong to disturb you.'

The man was already dressed, ready to creep out of the cottage. Eleanor had stretched out her arms, drawn him down to her. 'I love you,' she had told him, and clung to him while he stroked her hair.

'I have to go,' he had apologised and eventually, she had released him.

'We must do this again,' she had suggested, giggling. 'Soon.'

'Soon,' he echoed.

Eleanor remembered it with a warm, rueful satisfaction. Actually, that morning she had felt old and not a little mis-used but wholly, shamelessly without a regret in the world. However, as for making love 'again', at the time she had been far, far too sore to seriously entertain the notion of doing it again 'soon'. Or for several days thereafter. None of which mattered one iota, nor the fact she had seen Adam only fleetingly since that night. In a fortnight they would be married and away, together, looking forward to a new beginning. Afterwards, he would be posted off ops: he would be safe.

The radio announcer's clipped tones broke into her reverie.

"*The Air Ministry has issued the following Official Communiqué...*" Eleanor held her breath. "*Last night aircraft of Bomber Command were over Germany in great strength. The main objective was Brunswick. Other aircraft attacked targets in northern France, and mines were laid in enemy waters. Thirty-eight of our aircraft are missing...*"

Chapter 13

Saturday 15th January, 1944
RAF Ansham Wolds, Lincolnshire

Group Captain Pat Farlane went in search of his Squadron Commander on his return from Bawtry Hall. Apart from the chance encounter with Eleanor his first full day in command at Ansham Wolds had not been a happy one. A series of interviews and briefings with section heads and specialists at Group Headquarters had done nothing to elevate his spirits in the aftermath of the Brunswick fiasco. To add insult to injury the AOC had kept him cooling his heels for over an hour for the privilege of a completely unnecessary five minute exhortation on the subject of making sure that, quote: 'The crews press on!'

He found Adam in his office.

"Don't get up," he growled, limping in. "I hear the chaps are having a wake in the mess tonight?"

"Part wake, part a belated stag party, sir."

"Stag party?" Queried the older man, pulling up a chair and gratefully, wearily slumping onto it.

"Peter Tilliard's navigator got hitched today. Registry Office job in Scunthorpe. Jack Gordon. He's an Aussie, a bit of a rough diamond. I've recommended him for Navigation Leader, actually. I put his promotion papers on your desk. He's a good sort. The best, in fact. Married a local girl from Kingston Magna. A publican's daughter, I believe."

Adam leaned across his desk, proffering his

silver cigarette case. Farlane looked at it, recognised it and the monogram within.

"Isn't that Helen's?"

"I know. I know. If I was an officer and a gentleman I'd throw it away," he shrugged. "But it has kept me safe so far."

Farlane did not dispute it. Even a man like Adam Chantrey was allowed his superstitions.

"I met Eleanor today," he said. "When I popped down to the church to pay my respects to Bert. She was there. Introduced herself. Charming woman. Enchanting. Obviously, much too good for you!"

"That's what I told the Prof, sir," Adam confessed, dryly. He came around the desk, struck a match and lit his Station Commander's cigarette.

"Adam, old son," Pat murmured. "Be a good fellow, drop this 'sir' nonsense, in private. There's a good fellow."

"As you wish."

"Unless of course we're having a good old-fashioned row about something," laughed the older man. "In which case I reserve the right to pull rank whenever it suits me."

Adam laughed with him.

"Sounds fair enough to me."

"Good. The AOC is in the process of sending out orders to the effect that in future whenever our gunners spot a fighter they are to open fire immediately." It was said with an ill-disguised contempt.

The bombshell struck Adam speechless. He was about to protest: "Over my dead body!" When his friend cut him short.

"The AOC, in his wisdom," he went on, sarcastically, "is of the opinion that it is about time we 'carried' the fight to the Luftwaffe. The Ops Section is all in favour of a change in policy. Freddie Tomlinson was as keen as mustard about it."

"Command won't stand for it! Surely, they won't?"

"Command?" The Station Master scoffed, disgustedly. "Command doesn't have a position on it. According to Freddie the Pathfinders are dead against it, but that doesn't cut much ice right now." He sighed. "While we're on the subject, Eight Group didn't exactly cover themselves with glory last night. 'Shambles' was the word the ops people were using."

Adam thought that was a little unfair.

"Somebody at Command got the winds wrong, that's all," he commented, neutrally. "None of us liked that long leg in to the target. There was nothing between Celle and Brunswick likely to show up on *H2S*. The Pathfinders probably did the best they could in the circumstances."

Once again the openers had taken a beating on the way to Brunswick; at least 10 of the missing Lancasters were Pathfinders. Some of the things that were being said about the Pathfinders left a bad taste in Adam's mouth. Even as 8 Group pressed on over Germany the true believers – the majority safely flying their desks in England - were looking for scapegoats, sharpening their knives. It was a disgrace. Nobody at Command seemed to recognise what was staring them in the face. The only question that actually mattered was whether or not, given their recent heavy casualties and the flawed tools at their disposal, the Pathfinders were simply being asked to do too much?

"The Pathfinders put their markers down three or four miles south of the A.P," Adam remarked, trying to put things in perspective. "Over the Big City, that would have been pretty good going. Unfortunately, over a smaller target like Brunswick it meant most of the bombing went down in open country."

"It's a scandal!"

"These things happen."

"They bloody well shouldn't happen!"

Adam said nothing. People tended to take Pat Farlane's Devil may care, easy going manner at face value. However, beneath the jovial exterior there lurked the soul of a true 'press on' merchant. He was a man who had fought his way back from terrible injuries and come home at last to the squadrons he loved. Pat was a man in a hurry. A driven man.

"Three kites lost," he fumed. "For what?"

Adam judged it politic to remain silent. The fighters had worked the route all the way out, swarmed in the night over Brunswick. The crews reported constant combats, aircraft blowing up, falling in flames. The multi-coloured funeral pyres of Pathfinders burning on the Saxon plain had marked the route across Germany. In the grim perspective of the bombing war 38 missing heavies would have been a fair price to pay for the razing of another city. As it was three more of his crews were gone. Gone, most likely dead for nothing.

"Still no news of our lost sheep?" Pat inquired,

calming.

Adam shook his head. Earlier that evening he had signed twenty-one letters to next-of-kin. As if to advertise the lottery of life and death in the bomber streams over Germany, between them the three missing crews had completed over fifty operations.

"Have you made up your mind about Messingham Priory?" His friend inquired.

Adam stubbed out the butt of his cigarette, half-smiled.

"I'm game if you are."

"Good show." Pat smiled broadly. "That's what I hoped you'd say. Drop what you're doing, this calls for a drink."

Chapter 14

Tuesday 18th January, 1944
The Gatekeeper's Lodge, Ansham Wolds, Lincolnshire

Eleanor left the two men talking shop by the fire. Rufus followed her into the kitchen, nudged her knee, looked up hopefully. She gazed at the dog and the Alsatian wagged his tail.

She heard Pat Farlane laughing, Adam's laconic tones, and understood exactly how it was that so many women felt excluded in the company of the men they loved, irrationally jealous of the unique intimacy of comrades in arms. Adam and Pat could have been brothers. In a way they were brothers.

Eleanor took pity on Rufus and put the empty stewing pot on the floor. The dog pinned it down with one huge paw and thrust his big, black snout deep into it, licking enthusiastically, as if there was no tomorrow. Leaving her future husband's pet wolf to clean out the pot, she filled the kettle and stepped into the larder. This, she decided, was definitely the occasion for the last of her Darjeeling and for a rare airing of her best china tea set.

Adam had despatched the Station Master's WAAF driver, an ungainly, jolly girl, to the school at lunchtime with a note asking if it would be convenient for him to call with Pat that evening. *'Just a social call - for goodness sake don't go putting yourself out, my love.'* Eleanor had sent back a message inviting them to dinner. She collected up the cups and saucers, arranged them on the tray. The men's voices carried through the open door.

They were reminiscing about Boscombe Down when she returned with the tea tray. Adam took it out of her hands while she settled, kneeling by his chair. She had sat the men in the two armchairs to keep them from getting under her feet. Laying the tray on the rug, she poured the tea.

"Tell me, Pat," Eleanor prompted, smiling a wry smile. "Father called the Boscombe Down pilots the 'four musketeers'? Adam's terrible. He's told me that Dave was D'Artagnon, but he won't admit which one he was?"

Pat Farlane laughed heartily.

"My, that's a difficult one!" He paused for a moment's earnest, very exaggerated contemplation, his brow furrowing theatrically. "Well, Dave would certainly have been D'Artagnon. Every inch the headstrong young Gascon out to make a name for himself in the imperial service. Bill Simmons? Porthos, I think. A great-hearted fellow, brave as a lion. Utterly fearless. As for Max Reville? Athos, methinks. The gentleman soldier and courtier, no more gallant, kinder man anywhere in Christendom. Now, if I remember my Dumas, I think that just leaves Aramis, doesn't it?"

"Aramis," Eleanor said, the word rolling poetically, whimsically off her tongue. "Of course, Aramis." Aramis, the solemn knightly warrior who dressed in black and dreamed of a life of simple piety far from the fields of valour. Aramis, the despiser of vainglory. "Yes, Aramis."

"It suits him well!" Pat declared. "Don't you

think?"

Adam shook his head, laughed.

"I'm not at all sure I care to be cast in the role of some latter-day Templar," he objected, mildly.

Pat clasped his hands on his lap, sighed contentedly as he viewed his friend and Eleanor. The woman radiated calm and Adam was in her thrall. If only his crews could see him now, he thought to himself. To his crews Adam Chantrey was an enigmatic, solitary, charismatic figure, old before his time. Yet in Eleanor's presence the worry lines faded and the years fell off him. The hard-bitten old lag grinned boyishly, infectiously. At such times he was betrayed only by the faded ribbons on his battledress and the hollowness that lingered occasionally in his grey blue eyes.

"My word," he grimaced, realising he was getting sentimental. Eleanor, the cottage, home cooking, the chance to weave a story for the benefit of his host's children, tea and good company - the very best of company - beside a blazing fire, had filled him with an immense sense of well-being. "This is the life, what!"

"More tea?" Eleanor asked.

"Just the ticket, thank you. Adam was telling me you might go down to the West Country after the wedding?"

She nodded, poured more tea.

"Adam's sister, Henrietta, has asked us down to Tavistock."

"Dartmoor, bit bleak at this time of year?"

"Henrietta says her children are looking forward to meeting Johnny and Emmy," Eleanor told him. "It sounds lovely down there."

Adam listened with half an ear. He had not known what to expect when he wrote to Henrietta to tell her his news, half-hoping she would pass it on to the various far-flung members of the family. His sister, the only member of the clan with whom he regularly corresponded, had rattled back a short, bright letter of congratulation containing a sealed enclosure addressed to *"The Future Mrs Chantrey"*. Eleanor had read her letter, her expression one of happy curiosity. When she had finished reading she had smiled sweetly, folded it, and placed it in her apron pocket. "We shall stay at Tavistock, then," she had announced, settling matters.

"You'll get on splendidly with Hen," Pat assured the woman. "She's a good sport. Doesn't take any nonsense from anybody."

"That's Hen," Adam confirmed, a little sheepishly.

Around ten the men got up to go. Pat took Eleanor's hand, kissed it. She pecked him on the cheek and he coloured.

"You're always welcome, Pat," she told him.

"Thank you for putting up with me, dear lady." He stuttered, edging towards the Bentley, briefly leaving the betrothed couple together on the door step.

"Thursday?" Eleanor whispered.

The lovers eyes met in the darkness, they kissed.

"Yes. Thursday."

Eleanor waved and Adam was gone.

Chapter 15

Thursday 20th January, 1944
Lancaster B-Beer, 5 miles East of Wittstock

Jack Gordon watched the southern shore of the Muritzee Lake slide slowly off the top of the flickering, pulsing tube of the *H2S* screen. The flight out had been uneventful, routine. The gunners had reported a few combats, nothing out of the ordinary. Command had routed the bomber stream north through the Hamburg - Kiel gap; and abandoning the normal straight-in route seemed to have avoided a repeat of the Brunswick bloodbath. So far so good, there was nothing to suggest this had the makings of a bad night, thus far it was exactly what the new Mrs Gordon would have ordered.

Jack tried not to think about the new Mrs Gordon when he was in the air. Thoughts about the new Mrs Gordon were too distracting. Too distracting by far. The new Mrs Gordon had been beside herself when he broke the news the Wingco had put him forward for Navigation Leader. He had been more than somewhat chuffed himself, although at enormous pains to conceal the fact. Especially, from the Wingco.

'Does that mean you'll be a Squadron Leader?' Nancy had demanded, hugging him ecstatically.

'It's down to the new Station Master whether I get put forward for promotion. I might even have to go up to Group for a board,' he had explained, struggling not to look too pleased with himself.

'But Nav Leaders on three-flight squadrons tend to be Squadron Leaders, these days.'

Nancy had vented a loud, high-pitched squeal of delight and rushed off to tell her mother, father, miscellaneous siblings and the regulars in the bar the glad tidings. His memory of subsequent events was a little hazy.

That was last night. This morning, when Jack had gazed, bleary-eyed out of the window of the attic bedroom of the *Hare and Hounds* his thick head had cleared in an instant. The cloud and rain of recent days had blown away, the sky was cold, bright and still. Ops weather. Nancy had propped herself up in the bed.

'You're not going straight off, Jack?'

'Afraid so, my lovely.'

Throwing off the blankets, she had swung her feet of the bed and snatched up her robe from the chair by the door.

'At least let me make you your breakfast.'

'Sorry, no time.'

'Jack!'

'Ops weather, my lovely,' he apologised, forcing a smile. 'I can't keep the chaps waiting, can I now?'

'Oh, Jack!' Nancy had pleaded. Her long blond hair was tangled, alluringly awry, and her crumpled nightdress tantalisingly advertised the luscious, warm curves beneath. He had almost weakened. A kiss, a single tight, moaning hug and he had fled into the wintery dawn before he was imprisoned by Nancy's tears. He would make it up to her one day. He would make it up to her if it was the last thing he did.

One day he would make everything right.

Jack stared intently at the *H2S* screen.

"Navigator to pilot," he called over the intercom.

"Yes, Jack," Peter Tilliard drawled, amiably.

"We're spot on track, skipper. Hold on one-six-oh. ETA over the Berlin defended zone in about nine minutes."

"Steer one-six-oh," the pilot acknowledged.

The shoreline of the Muritzee Lake disappeared off the scope to be replaced by the finer, confused tracery of the marshy water lands to the south. The navigator methodically plotted ground features against these blurred, grainy forms. B-Beer's ground track crept down the chart ever nearer the huge, terrifying barrier of the Big City. The Lancaster shuddered as it crossed the backwash of another, unseen heavy's passage. A minute later the rear gunner reported a combat.

"Flamer going down at seven o'clock. Range five miles." Then, tersely: "No flak, must have been a fighter."

Jack noted the report, marked the chart. Probably a Halifax.

The new Mrs Gordon had wanted a church wedding, a white wedding in Ansham Wolds. It was not to be. The banns had been read the first week, then the Rector had visited Bill Bowman. Apparently, the old man was very civil, albeit in a stuffed-shirt sort of way but the upshot had been that he was not prepared to conduct the marriage. There would be no church wedding. Word had reached the Reverend about Nancy's 'condition', and in the circumstances, he felt it was no longer 'appropriate' for him to marry them in his church.

Peter Tilliard had called in at the Rectory to remonstrate on Jack's behalf, but the Vicar had been adamant.

'Sorry, Jack,' Peter had reported. 'He won't wear it, I'm afraid. The funniest thing was I got the distinct impression he was as upset about it as me. Do you want me to have a word with the Wingco?'

'No, thanks,' Jack had said, instantly, without thinking. He regretted it now. Perhaps, the Wingco might have been able to get the Rector to see sense. If anybody could, he would have been the man to do it.

He had married Nancy in Scunthorpe Registry Office. Peter Tilliard had been his best man. Nancy deserved a white wedding, a proper church wedding. He had not even been able to give her that. One day he would make it up to her. He swore he would make it up to her. Whatever happened, he would make it up to her. But first he had to survive.

"Searchlights and flak up ahead," Tilliard announced, cheerfully. "Eyes peeled, chaps. The Luftwaffe are bound to be around here somewhere."

Unbidden, Jack switched off the *H2S* set, clambered up to the cockpit, wedged himself in the astrodome, reconnected his oxygen line, plugged himself into the intercom circuit and began to scan the night. His 10-centimetre *H2S* was useless over Berlin, the screen a whiteout of ground returns. Tonight, his eyes would be better employed looking for fighters. The city was somewhere under the clouds twenty-two thousand feet below. Hundreds of searchlights played on the underside of the clouds perfectly silhouetting the river of heavies flowing, droning slowly across it. B-Beer rocked, bumped through the first line of flak. Up ahead the night sparkled evilly as shells exploded murderously in the path of the bomber stream. Sky Markers drifted over the city, target indicators went down, incandescent red balls of fire, dripping, showering tendrils of flame. A line of fighter flares ignited in the eastern sky, more Sky Markers fell in the south. Yellow and red TIs sank into the clouds, and were snuffed out in an instant. Hundreds of heavies were over Berlin, cookies and incendiaries were spilling from the bellies of the openers. There was no sound but the roar of the Merlins and the occasional rattle of spent shrapnel on the fuselage. Cookies struck ground in the streets, hundreds of guns filled the night with death and yet there was no sound. The clouds shook, giant shockwaves rippled, the fires in the streets began to glow. Huge fires were burning in those streets, bomb loads were scattering across Berlin. The openers had done their job and now it was up to the Main Force to press on. Several groups of Sky Markers were visible and B-Beer was running in to bomb the nearest. It was like a waking dream, as if he was a stranger sleepwalking through a world gone mad. Jack listened to the bomb-aimer's running commentary.

"Right a bit. Steady. Steady." Billy Campbell was glued to the bombsight. Young Billy was a stickler for actually bombing 'something'. If he could not find something recognisable on the ground to bomb, he always tried to hit a Sky Marker. "Left a bit. Left. Steady. Steady."

A mile away, and directly ahead an aircraft blew up. Jack was watching it when it happened. There was no tracer, no flak. One moment the bomber was flying along, the next it was a ball of fire, plummeting earthward.

"BOMBS GONE!" Billy yelled, rather unnecessarily. Free of her burden B-Beer reared up, surged forward. Immediately, Peter Tilliard put the nose down, advanced the throttles. There was ten-tenths cloud from horizon to horizon and therefore no profit in hanging around to get a print of the AP. Common sense dictated they get out of the target area as quickly as possible. Jack saw another heavy falling in the distance.

Then another.

The fighters had belatedly joined the party.

Chapter 16

Friday 21st January, 1944
RAF Waltham Grange, Lincolnshire

The first Lancasters got back a little after midnight. Thirty minutes later a dozen aircraft were orbiting the airfield, awaiting their turn to land. Soon the crews began to file wearily into the Briefing Hall. When the CO's crew made its entrance there was a quickening of the banter among the other crews, and a deal of back-slapping. Wing-Commander Clive Irving, resplendent in his sheepskins, cigarette in hand strolled from crew to crew, chatting, questioning, joking. It was nearly two o'clock before he cajoled his own crew down to the end of the room where the debriefers had arranged their tables.

"How's my favourite debriefer?" He asked Suzy, who blushed deeply.

"Very well. Thank you, sir," she murmured, unnerved not so much by the CO's noisy, brash bonhomie, to which she had become accustomed, but by the dark, smiling eyes of Irving's Canadian navigator. Flying Officer Don McNeill was two years older than her, quietly spoken, from Ottawa. Don had already asked her out twice.

"Jolly good!" Irving boomed, rubbing his hands together.

Suzy was at pains to avoid McNeill's eye. She assumed the Canadian had guessed about her and Peter Tilliard, and knew that it was over. A thing of the past. Notwithstanding, her eyes had inadvertently met Don McNeill's across more than one crowded room in the last fortnight.

'How about taking in a film in Lincoln one night?' He had suggested out of the blue, on Monday. No preamble, no small talk. He had just come out with it, startled her. Then yesterday they had bumped into each other, literally, outside the Operations Room. 'Have you thought any more about what I said the other day?'

'What was that?'

'A film?' He had smiled. 'In Lincoln?'

'Oh, that...'

'Or we could go for a drink somewhere? A meal if you like? It's up to you. We could go for a walk? A drive? Why not a drive? Forget the film. We won't have a drink, either. Or anything to eat. We could just drive somewhere, not eat anything? Or drink anything? We could just sit in the car and sort of ignore each other?'

Suzy's guard had slipped. She had laughed.

'No, thank you. I'd rather not, if it's all the same. Thank you for asking, anyway.'

Don McNeill had not been offended, taken this in his stride.

'Another time, maybe?'

'Maybe,' she had echoed.

Suzy forced herself to ignore Don McNeill's dark eyes. She focussed on the business in hand. The accounts of earlier crews were beginning to coalesce into a coherent picture of events over Germany. The bomber stream had reached the target more or less intact and the Pathfinders had got the attack off to an unusually good start. Thereafter, things had slowly, inexorably gone awry. The marking had become scattered and so had the bombing effort, mainly because of the ferocity of the flak. As many as a dozen aircraft had gone down over Berlin and later the fighters had worked the route all the way back to the Dutch coast. A frighteningly large number of bombers had been shot down on the way home.

Irving liked to hang back until most of his crews had been debriefed. He listened thoughtfully to Suzy's concise summation. The Intelligence Officer came over and pulled up a chair, saying nothing.

"We had a bit of a run in with a fighter east of Lubeck," Irving prefaced. "Don will give you the exact position," he promised, winking at Suzy. "I think the other fellow must have been a beginner. He followed us for ages then came barrelling in like a maniac. He almost got himself shot down, silly sod. Anyway, we corkscrewed a couple of times and lost him. I think he must have stalled out trying to follow us down."

The Intelligence Officer frowned. The Group Commander had recently issued a standing order to the effect that fighters were to be engaged on sight, and he felt bound to ask, what to him, seemed the obvious question.

"Did you not attempt to engage the fighter, sir?"

"Don't be a clot!" Irving snapped, irascibly, regally dismissive. "Where was I?"

Suzy knew that Waltham Grange's old lags had decided amongst themselves, with their CO's tacit approval, to tacitly disregard the Group Commander's edict. No gunner in his right mind deliberately picked a fight with a night fighter. The

Group's Lancasters were armed with rifle calibre machine guns that were massively out-gunned and out-ranged by their adversaries. Shooting it out with a cannon-armed fighter was an absolute last resort.

"You corkscrewed a couple of times and lost him," Suzy prompted. "You must have lost a lot of height and time?"

"Too right. We managed to climb back up to about eighteen thousand feet to bomb but by then practically everybody else was on their way home. We ended up over Berlin in the middle of a gaggle of Halifaxes. Flak got one quite close to us. Saw a fighter knock down a couple more as we were leaving the target. Junkers Eighty-Eight, hundreds of aerials sticking out of his front end. It attacked one kite, set its wing tanks on fire. Then, cool as you like the beggar throttles back, goes up behind another one, blows him up with a two second burst." Irving clicked his fingers. "Just like that! Anyway, after that I pulled out all the stops and climbed up to twenty-three thousand feet. Damned unhealthy down among the Halifaxes!"

"Any sign of fires below the clouds, sir?" Suzy inquired, coolly.

"I should say!"

"All over the shop!" Chorused Clive Irving's gunners.

At four in the morning Suzy gathered up her notes and headed for the watchtower. There were reports to be written, returns to be checked and rechecked before dispatch to Group. Outside, the rain was falling steadily, soaking the grass. She hurried along the path, stepping between the puddles.

The sentry at the Ops Room door was talking to a second man, who detached himself, moved out of the shadows at her approach.

"Hi," said a familiar voice.

Suzy halted. "You should get some sleep," she admonished the man. "For all you know you could be operating again tonight."

"Maybe," Don McNeill agreed, chuckling. "Anyway, what about that film in Lincoln we were talking about?"

"We weren't talking about any such thing!"

"Just one film?"

Suzy was tired, very tired and getting wetter by the second. Before her lay many hours of work and he was stopping her getting on with it. He seemed a nice enough man. What harm would it do? One film. One evening in Lincoln. And then he would leave her alone.

"Oh, all right," she agreed, irritably.

Chapter 17

Friday 21st January, 1944
RAF Ansham Wolds, Lincolnshire

Last night the target had been Berlin. Tonight, the target was Magdeburg, an ancient Hanseatic city eighty miles west-south-west of the Big City on the banks of the River Elbe. The city was a railway and industrial centre situated at the eastern end of the Weser-Elbe Canal which on its opening just before the war, had linked Magdeburg via the Mitteland Canal to the factories of the Ruhr Valley. Bomber Command had not previously attacked Magdeburg in strength. Magdeburg was therefore, intact, undamaged.

Magdeburg, in translation a corruption of the Episcopal city's original Wendish name, Magataburg, meant 'the virgin city'. The city had been almost completely destroyed three hundred years ago in the Thirty Years War and now the Main Force planned to re-visit the horrors of that war upon it. Tonight, the Chief was hurling every available Lancaster and Halifax - some 650 heavies - at the virgin city.

Adam got to his feet to conclude the main crew briefing.

Maximum efforts to distant targets on successive nights taxed both men and machines to the limit. However, this evening, weariness was not the problem it often was in these situations. Most of the crews who had participated in the previous evening's Berlin op had got back around midnight and had had a good night's sleep. Moreover, notwithstanding the fact the Halifaxes, comprising a third of the force despatched to the Big City had suffered two-thirds of the casualties, the Chief was sending the Halifaxes back to Germany again tonight. Adam's crews were counting their blessings, their gripes were muted.

"Settle down, please," he called, clasping his trusty billiard cue. "Before I sum up I have an announcement to make." The crews were silent, hushed. "As you probably already know, Squadron Leader Barlow's aircraft failed to return from last night's op. Accordingly, Flight-Lieutenant Calder has assumed command of A Flight, effective as of twelve hundred hours this day."

Adam moved on swiftly. As always, time was pressing. Tonight, a variety of diversionary operations had been planned for the delectation of the defenders. The highlight being an attack by twenty-two 5 Group Lancasters and a dozen Pathfinder Mosquitoes on Berlin. He was at great pains to sound optimistic.

"The Berlin diversionary force will run into the target *Windowing* heavily, dropping lots of flares and TIs, attempting to mimic the beginning of a big raid," he told the crews. "It ought to be quite a fireworks display. In addition, there's a fair bit of activity elsewhere. Eight Group Mosquitoes will be mounting spoofs on Oberhausen and Duisburg, and Three Group's Stirlings are off to France."

Bombing French fields was about all the Stirlings were fit for, he reflected. Slow and with a maximum service ceiling of only around sixteen thousand feet the Stirling was a death trap over

Germany. Any day now the Halifaxes were likely to follow the Stirlings into the backwaters of the bombing war. To a lesser degree the Halifax - particularly the Mark V, which still equipped the majority of 4 and 6 (Royal Canadian Air Force) Groups - shared many of the deficiencies of the Stirling. Its performance was markedly inferior to that of the Lancaster, and worse, it was prone to fundamental mechanical defects that by and large, all three main production variants of the Lancaster, were not. Last night's carnage in the Halifax Force was only the latest in a series of brutal object lessons. Whenever the fighters appeared the Lancaster Force climbed higher leaving the Halifaxes to their fate.

"There will also be some OTU Wellingtons *Gardening* off the Biscay ports and *Nickeling* over northern France and Belgium," he continued, jaw jutting. Dropping propaganda leaflets - *Nickeling* - was the way Bomber Command had passed the first winter of the war. He recollected those far off days with incredulity in the light of what had followed. On his first trip to Berlin he had dropped a cargo of forged German food rationing coupons; recently, he had discovered that the Germans had not introduced rationing of any kind until two years later. "And of course, 100 Group will be sending intruders to stooge around the Dutch and north German fighter fields. All told, there will be over eight hundred aircraft in the air tonight."

The aiming point was near the cathedral.

An accident of history.

From four miles high at night it was virtually impossible to identify ground features, let alone individual buildings. Over Magdeburg his bomb-aimers would pray for a glimpse of the bend of the River Elbe, a well-placed TI, any sort of reference point would do. Over the target wise pilots gave their bomb-aimers licence to unload on the first half-decent concentration of TIs or Sky Markers that they stumbled across.

That afternoon Adam had called his own crew together one last time. When he had asked the chaps to fly one more op there had been no dissenters. The decision to fly one more op and to sign off with a flourish appealed to them all.

Adam would confront Pat Farlane's wrath in due course. The Station Master had been called to Bawtry Hall to 'discuss' the opening of Messingham Priory. With another Goodwood in the offing Pat had not been a very happy man that afternoon. He would be even unhappier still in the morning. In fact, his old friend would be livid. And rightly so. But that was tomorrow and tomorrow was a strange country.

In the meantime he meant to fly his one hundredth op.

Bert Fulshawe had made it into the eighties.

One of the survivors of the Wilhelmshaven raid owed it to the others to make it to a century. The war would be over before they let him back on ops. He would seize the day.

Today.

He would let the chaps in on the secret it was his hundredth op in the morning.

Afterwards, he would apologise to Pat Farlane.

"I'm taking the spare kite tonight," Adam had informed Bob Nicholson

Nicholson had nodded, left it at that. Stirling man, Halifax man, Lancaster man it was all the same. Once an ops man, always an ops man. Nicholson knew that there were things best not discussed, questions best left unasked. Understood that this was neither the time nor the place to make a scene, nor to remind the Wingco that officially he was grounded, pending posting.

"Good luck, sir."

"Thanks, Bob."

Chapter 18

Friday 21st January, 1944
Lancaster L-Lincoln, 60 Miles SE of Mablethorpe

L-Lincoln climbed out of the broken cloud into a black, empty sky. Adam was calm, now. Deadly calm. An hour ago he had seethed with rage. A sprog crew had put a wheel on the infield, bogged down and very nearly turned the off into a farce. The incident had blocked the perimeter road with 14 of his 22 heavies still waiting to take off. It had taken an age - some twenty minutes - to tow away the offending Lancaster.

L-Lincoln's *Gee* set had failed shortly after takeoff.

'Can you fix it, Ben?' He had inquired, casually.

'Ask me again when the fire's out, Skipper!' The navigator had retorted tersely.

It got worse. L-Lincoln was a valiant but aging warhorse. A sturdy aircraft with more than twenty ops to her credit she flew with her starboard wing low and no amount of trimming seemed to make the slightest difference.

Adam began to call around the crew stations.

"Pilot to navigator. Tell me some good news, please!"

"Sorry, Skipper. No can do!" Ben apologised, prior to reporting that *H2S* was also inoperable. "The circuit must have shorted when the *Gee* set caught alight."

Adam shrugged this off. They would press on.

"Never mind. We'll have to rely on the old-fashioned methods, then."

"Afraid so. I'll try to get a couple of star sights before we reach the convergence point, Skipper."

"Roger. Let me know when you're in position." Adam moved on. "Pilot to W/T op. How's your box of tricks, Bert?"

Flight Sergeant Bert Pound flicked his intercom switch.

"Everything is fine, Skipper." The W/T operator was already eavesdropping on the frequencies supplied by the operations officer. Over the course of two tours he had developed a finely tuned understanding for the habits of his enemies, a sixth sense that guided him with increasing certainty to the ever-changing frequencies of the fighter masters and their slaves. Departing from the narrow band of Group-assigned frequencies he picked up traffic almost immediately, lost it the next moment. Distant traffic, too distant to jam. Up ahead the fighters were climbing in the night over the Low Countries and north-western Germany. The battle was about to begin.

"Pilot to gunners," he heard the Skipper sing out. "Test your guns, please."

The Lancaster shuddered as the gunners fired off two second bursts.

Bert concentrated on his receiver. In twenty minutes he would retune, try to pick up the first 'found winds' broadcast. In the meantime he listened for guttural Germanic tongues through the hiss of the ether. Night fighters were marshalling around beacon Ludwig, south of Osnabruck. Unfortunately, as chance would have it, tonight the bomber stream was steering almost directly at the main concentration of fighters. The voices in the ether were distant but there seemed to him to be an awful lot of them. He tried hard not to think about the fighters swarming up to meet the Main Force over Saxony.

Many, many fighters.

Chapter 19

Friday 21st January, 1944
Lancaster L-Lincoln, 20 miles ENE of Hanover

It was one of those trips when navigation presented none of the usual problems. The night fighters got into the bomber stream as the openers crossed the Dutch coast, and thereafter, Main Force pilots set their course by the light of heavies burning on the ground. Pathfinders burned prettily. Halifaxes with their all-incendiary bomb loads burned brightly, almost as spectacularly although not with the varied multi-coloured hues of Pathfinders. Main Force Lancasters produced different kinds of fires on the ground. Often their cookies would detonate in the crash, scattering incendiaries over broad reaches of countryside, producing a diffuse, relatively short-lived spectacular circle of fire.

Hunched in the rear turret behind the sights of his four Browning machine guns Taffy Davies was a frightened man. He was accustomed to fear and to ignoring it. Fear was a thing you learned to live with. Fear was normal, nothing to be ashamed of but tonight he was unable to brush it aside, it constricted his throat, slowed his reflexes. In 51 ops he had seen plenty of heavies blowing up, falling in flames, tumbling broken, disintegrating, spewing burning 100-octane, TIs and incendiaries all the way to the ground. You expected to see kites going down. But not all the time. What was going on tonight was something wholly out of the ordinary. Too many heavies were falling. There were too many combats, too many kites just blowing up.

"Exploding heavy at eight o'clock, range three miles," he grated through clenched teeth. "No tracer, no combat. It just blew up." It was the third kite he had seen blow up in mid-air without warning in the last ten minutes. Then: "Combat at four o'clock, range five miles. Fighter attack from astern, I saw the tracer. Kite burning, going down." He and Bob Marshall in the mid-upper turret, had reported combats and kites going down all the way from the coast. They were witnessing a disaster. Something had gone wrong, terribly wrong. What was unfolding around them was not war, it was cold-blooded murder.

Taffy traversed his turret from one beam to the other without a pause, quartering the sky. The Skipper's words always came back to him on a bad night. In the early days, the Skipper had harangued his gunners about night fighter tactics. Before each operation he would take each gunner aside, ram home the message. Taffy used to listen with no more than half an ear.

'A fighter starts with four advantages,' the Skipper had drummed into him. 'Speed, manoeuvrability, fire-power and most important, the initiative. To survive we must use the fighter's speed and manoeuvrability against it, deny it the opportunity to use its superior fire-power, and we *must* seize the initiative.' To start with Taffy had blinked at him in bafflement. Then the Skipper had instructed him on the workings of a fighter pilot's mind, and in what he described as 'the rules of the game'.

'A night fighter will attempt to approach its target from the target's area of maximum invisibility. This will be either the darkest part of the sky, or a target's known blind spot. In the case of our heavies, that means from below. Ideally, a fighter will close with its target relatively slowly to reduce the odds of overshooting if the target makes a sudden course change. The fighter's angle of approach will be as direct as possible consistent with the fighter pilot's perception of what we might call his 'avenue of maximum invisibility'. If a target is weaving about then the fighter's avenue of maximum invisibility will be drastically reduced and the fighter pilot has to allow for this. Usually, this will mean he has to attempt to close with his target a lot faster than he really wants to. Depending on conditions, a fighter will hold its fire until it is within two hundred yards, often much less. You know yourself that deflection can be hellishly difficult to judge at night, so most fighter pilots will want to get into a position below a heavy, or failing that more or less dead astern before opening fire. Point blank range for a cannon armed night fighter is probably one hundred to one hundred and fifty yards on most nights.'

The Skipper usually paused for air at this point. But not for long. The Skipper was relentless. Until that was, he was satisfied a chap was on his wavelength.

'An old hand will squeeze off a two-second burst and break away. You'll know if you're up against a novice straight away because he'll open up at three or even four hundred yards and keep on shooting. An old hand won't open fire until he's damned sure he's close enough to get the job done with a single, short burst. An old hand will direct his fire into a heavy's wing roots. Not I hasten to say, out of compassion for the likes of you and I. But because experience will have taught an old hand that all it takes is a single cannon shell in a fuel tank and its curtains for any heavy. An old hand will also want plenty of time to get out of the way before the target blows up. A real expert will open fire and break away almost in the same manoeuvre, probably towards and underneath his target. Turning away from a target opens up a wider arc of fire for a target's gunners, so it's much better from the fighter's point of view to dive under a heavy before he breaks away.'

It was the sort of food for thought that turned a man's stomach. Nevertheless, Taffy had digested it whole and taken the Skipper's words of wisdom to heart.

'To have any chance of surviving a night fighter attack a Lanc must use the fighter's speed and nimbleness against it and seize the initiative. So, rule number one is that if you spot a fighter the last thing you do is open fire on it. It's a waste of time trying to shoot it out with a cannon-armed fighter. Shooting it out is an act of absolute last resort. Remember, a well-handled fighter always has the option of standing off and shooting us to bits without ever coming within the effective range of our Brownings.'

The Skipper was full of little rib-ticklers like that.

'So, if you spot a fighter, or more to the point, *anything* that could possibly be a fighter what you do is shout CORKSCREW at the top of your voice. Clear?'

The Skipper's gunners tended to nod at this stage.

'If you shout CORKSCREW at me I will always assume we have company. The sort of company that we have to get away from in a screaming hurry. When you shout CORKSCREW you will also shout either PORT or STARBOARD. Whether you shout PORT or STARBOARD will depend on which side of the aircraft the fighter is attacking from. You will always tell me to corkscrew *towards* the fighter. ALWAYS. No exceptions. Turning into an attacking fighter maximises the fighter's interception speed, reduces his aiming and shooting time and will tend to exaggerate his overshoot. Once we're under attack the object of the exercise is *not*, repeat NOT, to shoot the fighter down. We've got next to no chance of doing that. The object of the exercise is to run away. But before we can run away we have to make the beggar overshoot. Savvy?'

The Skipper was mad, of course. Barking mad. Seventy-nine fucking 'official' ops mad and probably a couple of dozen more 'unofficial' ops madder. Taffy went on staring into the night. The Skipper was calling around the crew stations. It was his periodic check to ensure that everybody was awake and that nobody's oxygen supply had failed.

"Pilot to rear gunner."

"Rear gunner to pilot," Taffy acknowledged, his teeth chattering. There was ice on the inside of the turret and despite his layers of clothing - thermal underwear, battledress, sweaters, fur-lined flying boots, and electrically-heated suit - he could no longer feel his feet, his hands were numb and the intensity of the cold was making him drowsy. "It's bloody freezing back here, Skipper!"

He shook his head.

He saw it in a moment.

He thought he was imagining it, hesitated.

There it was again: a speck of black against the darkness of the sky. Something wholly black and utterly malevolent glimpsed once and immediately lost in the impenetrable coal-cellar, ebony backdrop of the German night. Desperately, he strained to find it again. Whatever he had seen, it was exactly where he would expect a night fighter to be. Astern, lurking in the middle distance down in the inky blind zone between the horizon and the faint, sparsely spread stars high above.

His eyes found only blackness.

Every instinct cried out that there was something deadly in the darkness, roaring in for the kill. Still he saw nothing. And still he hesitated. Ragged nerve endings tingled.

Too late. It was already too late. He screamed into the intercom.

"CORKSCREW PORT! CORKSCREW PORT! GO! GO! GO!"

Blind terror paralysed his hands on the triggers of his guns as the Lancaster's port wing dropped sickeningly into the void. Taffy stared at the muzzle-flashes of the fighter's cannon, watched transfixed as the tracers fell in towards him, flying at impossible speeds directly above his head. The muzzle flashes of the fighter's cannons drifted across his gun sights. Blue-white tracer tore off the top of the turret, shells thudded into L-Lincoln's tail.

The turret jammed, traversed thirty degrees to port.

The intercom was dead.

The blood trickling down from his scalp froze on Taffy's face and oxygen mask as the slipstream whipped into the shattered turret. His air line severed, the dazed gunner was strangely unafraid as L-Lincoln fell out of the sky. Four miles high and starved of oxygen, blind terror, hopelessness, despair and an awful feeling of having let the crew down, slowly, surely dissolved into painless oblivion.

Chapter 20

Friday 21st January, 1944
Lancaster L-Lincoln, 5 Miles NE of Celle

Briefly, terrifyingly Adam had lost control of the bomber. Slamming the starboard throttles through the gate, pointing L-Lincoln's port wing tip at the ground the aircraft had fallen headlong into the darkness. The violence of the manoeuvre had almost ripped off the wings and precipitated a near vertical dive. Hanging in his straps he had wrestled with the controls for an eternity before anything had happened, before the Lancaster had begun to pull up. Eventually, he levelled out at eight thousand feet. In the great scheme of things, trading thirteen thousand feet of altitude for their lives was a fair trade.

Adam had felt the impact of cannon shells through the control column, glimpsed the tracers arching over the top of the cockpit. A novice randomly hosing bullets across the sky, he had concluded. The cold sweat dripped off his brow. An absolute beginner. A sprog night fighter pilot. Thank God! He flicked his intercom switch.

"Where'd that bloody fighter go?"

"Right over the top of us, Skipper," sang out Bob Marshall, shakily. "Junkers Eighty-Eight with a whole lot of aerials sticking out of its nose. Thought he was going to hit us, Skipper! He must have been right under the tail. He pulled up and went down to starboard. I think he stalled out avoiding collision."

"Pilot to rear gunner!" Adam called, irritably. "Are you still with us, Taffy? Talk to me you bolshie little basket!"

There was no reply.

The initial rush of adrenalin had abated now and Adam was suddenly aware of how stiff and heavy, leaden the controls had become. L-Lincoln was labouring, wallowing across the sky like a drunken matelot on his way back to his ship after a night on the town. The Merlins sounded healthy but the Lancaster responded sulkily, sluggishly when he tested the elevators and rudders. It was then that he belatedly realised Ted Hallowes was not at his shoulder. He twisted around in his seat. The flight engineer was lying in a crumpled heap on the cockpit floor where he had been flung by the corkscrew.

"Get a grip!" He snarled silently to himself. "Get a grip!"

"Pilot to navigator," he drawled over the intercom, taking stock.

First things first: get the head count out of the way. Second: assess the damage. Third: make sure that the wounded are made as comfortable as possible. Fourth, fifth, six: get back, survive, live to fight another day.

"Pilot to navigator. Speak to me, please, Ben!"

"I'm okay, Skipper," the big man acknowledged groggily. "I think all the hits were aft of the main spar."

"That's what it feels like up here," Adam agreed, matter of factly. "Bert, how are you? Still in one piece, I hope?"

"Yes, Skipper."

"Good. See what you can do for Ted. I think he took a bit of a wallop when we corkscrewed." He tried not to contemplate Taffy Davies's silence from the rear turret. "Pilot to bomb-aimer. Are you still with us, Round Again?"

"Yes, Skipper." Round Again did not sound convinced.

Adam mouthed a quick, no nonsense prayer for hydraulic pressure, and yanked on the bomb bay doors lever. L-Lincoln shuddered as the bomb bay doors swung open: one prayer at least answered.

"Pilot to bomb-aimer," he barked. "Jettison all bombs."

"Say again, Skipper?" Round Again was dazed, groggy.

"Jettison the bombs! NOW!"

"Oh, roger, Skipper."

The Lancaster reared up, staggered higher, and her over-strained airframe creaked a little less. She flew a little less sulkily.

"Bombs jettisoned!" Round Again shouted, watching the lights on his board winking out. Notwithstanding the situation, it was obvious from his tone that he was mortified to be dumping a perfectly good cookie and a full cargo of incendiaries on open countryside.

"Pilot to navigator," Adam called. "Plot me a course for home, Ben. Back the way we came in. Until I can think of something better, anyway!"

Ben had anticipated the request.

"Try three-oh-oh to be getting on with, Skipper," he suggested, unhesitatingly. "I'm off aft to see what's happened to Taffy, over."

"Understood. Keep me informed, out." Adam

pushed, prompted, nudging L-Lincoln's nose around to the north west. Lone bombers were meat and drink to the hunters. Cut out of the bomber stream a straggler was naked in the German night without the protection of *Window*. He started to lose height, mindful not to impose undue stress on the bomber's mishandled airframe. The best policy in these situations was to get down low, under the horizons of the magic eyes of the German search radars.

"Pilot to mid-upper gunner. Eyes peeled, Bob. We're relying on you to keep us out of trouble, now."

"Roger, Skipper." The skinny boy gunner in the Fraser Nash Type 50 turret sounded like the calmest man onboard. Not for the first time Adam was struck by young Bob Marshall's coolness under fire. A gauche, clumsy child on the ground, he had time and again demonstrated a steadiness under fire that put his elders to shame.

"Round Again, are you okay?" Adam re-checked.

"Yes, Skipper." The bomb-aimer was still not convinced. "I think I whacked my head on something," the Scot admitted. "Blacked out for a second. But I think I'm okay, Skipper."

"Right. Come up here and make yourself useful as an extra pair of eyes."

Adam tried not to think about what Ben would find in the rear turret, tried not to think about Mac's gunner being washed out of his turret with a fire hose.

"Combat astern one o'clock. Flamer going down!" Reported the mid-upper gunner. "Range five miles."

Another straggler. There would be many stragglers tonight. Stragglers like L-Lincoln, mauled by a fighter, limping home with dead and wounded onboard.

Chapter 21

Friday 21st January, 1944
Lancaster L-Lincoln, 20 Miles ESE of Bremen

Ben hauled his large, bruised frame over the main spar, past the trunking of the mid-upper turret searching for damage as he went by the light of his torch, dreading what awaited him in the rear turret.

There was little visible damage forward of the tail plane assembly. The Elsan chemical toilet had taken a direct hit, probably a ricochet off the ammunition ducts. Its remains littered the floor and the stench of it mingled with that of burnt cordite, leaking hydraulic fluid and scorched wiring. Another cannon shell had exploded against the starboard ammunition ducts, and bullets rolled underfoot in the effluent from the Elsan. Kicking through the debris Ben crawled onto the visibly warped walkway over the tail plane spar, and tried to pull open the draught-proof doors to gain access to the turret on the other side. The doors were deformed, bent. The whole tail section seemed to be twisted. Not good! Still, no point worrying about it. If the tail fell off, it fell off. There was bugger all he could do about it. Grunting with the effort, he grasped the door handles, forced them open. The slipstream ripped past him, frozen, thunderous, frightening.

He groaned when he saw the turret was traversed to starboard.

"Marvellous…"

L-Lincoln was in a shallow dive: right now they were in no man's land, sitting ducks. The Skipper was heading down to the deck.

The turret doors were jammed. He strained briefly to prise them apart but it was no good, he was unable to gain sufficient purchase. Cursing savagely, he squirmed forward over the tail plane walkway, ripped the fire axe from its stowage by the rear fuselage door and returned to the rear turret. Already sweating heavily from exertion despite the intensity of the cold, he wedged himself between the tail plane and the turret mounting ring, and began to hack at the metal where the doors met and locked. He could hardly see what he was doing. Sparks flew. Every few blows he halted, groped in the darkness, tested the growing gap until it was large enough to use the handle of the axe as a crow bar. The head of the axe came off the moment he leaned his full weight against the handle. He groaned out aloud, stuffing his gloved right hand into the jagged gap, pushed with his legs, hauled against the doors. A red haze descended on him. His bear-like strength was bleeding away, his breath came and went in short, ragged gulps. The frigid air seared his lungs. Time and again he tore at the immovable, mocking doors. Soon he would have to rest, re-gather his resources.

"Fuck it, you're not trying hard enough!" He scolded himself. Drove himself to greater efforts. "Harder! Harder!"

Taking a last, deep breath he planted his booted feet either side of the distorted frame, braced himself, threw his whole body against the doors in a final, despairing, immense levering movement. Nothing happened for a moment, then to his astonishment the doors buckled and flew open. He fell backwards, and ended up spread-eagled over the walkway.

Taffy was slumped over his guns and the top half of the turret had completely disappeared. Ben clambered into the back of the turret, pulled off the gunner's oxygen mask, unplugged his electrically heated flying suit, and released his straps. It was pointless trying to examine Taffy in the shattered turret. Without ceremony he grabbed the small, wiry gunner under the arms, took a firm grip and dragged the inert body backwards, out of the freezing, hurricane slipstream and out of the turret. Whatever Taffy's injuries, left in the raging cold of the turret he was a dead man. Manhandling the gunner as gently as circumstances permitted, he pulled him into the body of the fuselage. Forward of the mid-upper turret he laid his charge gently on the floor among the scattered bullets from the damaged ammunition trains.

Bert Pound leaned over the main spar, shone a torch.

"How is the little sod?"

"Dunno, yet!" Ben shouted against the roar of the slipstream.

"Ted's a bit groggy, but otherwise okay," the W/T operator yelled. "Round Again's gone back into the nose, he's map reading for the Skipper."

Ben crouched over the prostrate gunner, hurriedly inspecting him. There was a lot of blood on Taffy's face, its origin a nasty scalp wound.

This was his only visible injury. Unpleasant, but unlikely to prove fatal. The difficulty was in finding out if he had suffered any less obvious but more severe wounds. It was trial and error, a case of pushing and prodding. In the gloom of the mid-fuselage by torchlight it was a gruesome game of blind man's bluff. In these situations the main thing was always to establish if a man was bleeding to death, or not. Preferably, before he bought it. There was no time for niceties, for worrying about causing the wounded man unnecessary discomfort, let alone pain. The idea was to discover the worst quickly, and try to do something about it even faster.

"Tell the Skipper the rear turret's gone for a burton, Bert!" Ben bawled as his hands moved methodically, roughly under the gunner's sheepskins. Two tours, and nightmares every bit as grim as this one allowed him even now to think clearly, to remember the drill.

The drill was not to panic. The drill was to keep one's wits. The drill was to report to the Skipper. Do your job, and try not to shit yourself too often. Old lag's lore. No more, no less.

He continued his report: "One of the starboard ammo ducts is smashed up, there's loose ammo all over the place. The whole tail plane's a mess. Several twenty millimetre hits, big holes all over the shop. Tail plane spar looks a bit bent. The whole tail assembly looks like it's been knocked out of true. Make sure you warn the Skipper not to try any aerobatics. Off you go, Bert. Leave me the lamp."

The other man hesitated a moment. He too,

knew the drill.

"I'll be back in two ticks," he promised, scrambling forward into the darkness.

Ben straightened Taffy's unconscious form, sat back, shone the torch first on his left hand, then, hefting the torch from one hand to the other, the right. There was no blood on his hands. None at all which was amazingly good news. Better than he had dared to hope. His probing had discovered no broken bones under the gunner's sheepskins: or at least, nothing badly broken. He rose to his feet, walked, stumbled aft, crouching, collected the first aid box stowed next to the fuselage door, returned to Taffy, squeezing past the mid-upper turret.

The gunner's leather helmet was caked in blood. Ben hesitated before removing it, half-afraid the helmet might be all that was holding the gunner's skull together. In the end he decided that one way or another he had to find out the extent of the wound. They were a long way from home and before he shot Taffy full of morphine he had to know what he was dealing with. The gunner moaned as he studied the ugly, open wound. A shard of shrapnel, or perhaps, it might even have been a cannon shell, had ripped through the leather of the helmet and Taffy's scalp, down to the bone. Ben could see the white – a lot of white - of the exposed skull. Mercifully, there was no trace of anything foreign in the gaping three-inch wound. Ben groped for the intercom socket above the main spar, plugged himself in, flicked the switch.

"Navigator to pilot."

"Pilot to navigator."

"Taffy's got a head wound. Messy as hell, but he may be okay. I'm going to try and tidy him up a bit."

"Roger. Keep me informed."

Ben made no attempt to clean the wound, contented himself simply with wiping the worst of the blood away. He wanted to make sure it was the only wound. Satisfied, he applied a big, clumsy dressing to the gunner's scalp, winding a long bandage about his head. He had almost finished when the wounded man groaned loudly and blinked up at him in the gloom. Ben pinned Taffy's arms to the floor, guessing correctly that the gunner would panic, thrash around if he did not pin him down. The gunner squirmed feebly, eyes staring wildly.

"Calm down you clot, you're all right," Ben told him. "You're okay. Calm down, Taffy. You're okay."

The diminutive Welshman gave up the unequal struggle, lay still, breathing heavily.

"Fighter!" He gasped, voice strangled. "Fucking fighter!"

"Gone now! It's gone! We're on our way home."

Ben slowly released his iron grip, settled back on his haunches.

Grimacing, Taffy propped himself up on a shaky elbow.

"Didn't see it," he muttered. "Then it was there, close enough to fucking touch it was! Didn't see it!"

Ben patted his shoulder. "Doesn't matter, Taffy. Not your fault, old man."

"Didn't see the bastard!" With this, Taffy

started to be sick, violently and painfully. When he was finished Ben picked him up, moved him forward, propped him against the main spar. Vomit, effluent from the smashed Elsan and leaking hydraulic fluid washed about the floor of the fuselage, and more bullets from the shattered ammunition duct scattered into the evil, lapping pools.

The slipstream howled and whistled through the gaping holes in the tail as L-Lincoln limped into the west.

"Navigator to pilot," Ben reported. "Taffy's come round. Somebody ought to stay with him."

"Pilot to navigator," Adam drawled. "I'll send Round Again back to you."

"Roger, Skipper." Ben sighed. "Bloody stupid way to fight a war," he said to himself.

Chapter 22

Saturday 22nd January, 1944
Lancaster L-Lincoln, 6 Miles NE of Mablethorpe, Lincolnshire

Adam flicked the intercom switch. Ahead, the dim line of the coast was discernible every now and then through breaks in the cloud. He had been flying Ansham Wolds's base beam for ten minutes, homing in on safety and refuge. L-Lincoln wallowed about the sky, the rudder was virtually useless.

"Pilot to crew. Almost home chaps. Out."

"I hope somebody has the sense to turn on the Sandra lights, Skipper!" Ted Hallowes shouted in his ear.

Adam grinned wolfishly, glanced over his shoulder at the bloodied but unbowed figure of his Flight Engineer. The corkscrew had thrown Ted around the cockpit like a rag doll but he was a tough nut. When he came round he had shaken his head, refused all assistance, and staggered back to his position.

"We'll soon find out!"

As L-Lincoln slid leadenly over the Lincolnshire coast two thousand feet below he switched channels and called up the watchtower at Ansham Wolds.

"L-Lincoln to Chestnut control." The ether hissed and crackled. "L-Lincoln to Chestnut control," he intoned a second time, waited.

A woman's voice filtered faintly over the air:

"Hello L-Lincoln, this is Chestnut control."

"L-Lincoln to Chestnut control. Darkie. Repeat, darkie!"

The controller's voice remained level, unemotional.

"Hello L-Lincoln. Please confirm your position and the nature of your emergency."

"L-Lincoln to Chestnut control. Approximately five miles north of Manby." He hesitated, got his thoughts ordered. It was important to report what had happened. Just in case they did not make it. "We got shot up by a fighter – a Ju Eighty-Eight we think - somewhere between Bremen and Celle. Tail plane is a mess. No rudder control to speak of. Kite won't stay in trim. I don't know if we've got enough pressure to get the wheels down, or for the brakes. My rear gunner is wounded. Over."

"Understood, L-Lincoln. Pancake! Pancake! QFE one-zero-zero-nine, over."

"Roger, Chestnut Control. Pancake! QFE one-zero-zero-nine! Out!"

L-Lincoln crabbed on across the night as Adam flew the base beam. When the Lancaster slipped off the centreline of the runway the signal changed; to port the rhythm of the pulses quickened, to starboard they lengthened. He peered into the murky, inky darkness, searching, searching. The clouds parted and they flew into clear airs. In the distance three searchlights reached into the heavens.

"Looks like somebody remembered to turn on the Sandra lights, after all!" He yelled above the drone of the Merlins. "Let's start the drill, Ted."

"Auto-pilot control...OUT. Superchargers...IN

M RATIO. Air intake...SET TO COLD."

Then: "Brake pressure!"

"NO BRAKE PRESSURE!"

"Never mind!" Adam shouted. "Carry on!"

"Flaps...TWENTY DEGREES - DOWN ANGLE."

"Undercarriage!"

"DOWN!" Adam cursed to himself. The aircraft shuddered as the undercarriage creaked down into the slipstream. Normally, he felt the gear lock in place, tonight he did not.

"WARNING LIGHT!"

"Might just be the panel, Skipper!"

"Try the emergency air pressure bottle!"

Either the undercarriage was damaged or there was insufficient hydraulic pressure to properly extend it. The engineer scrambled aft. On newer aircraft the emergency air pressure lever was beside the engineer's panel, but on L-Lincoln the control was located behind the main spar.

"I heard the air go into the system, Skipper!" Hallowes reported on his return, breathlessly. He eyed the red warning light, blinking stubbornly, mockingly. "Must be the panel! Must be!"

"Must be! We'll have to take our chances," Adam decided. "I don't fancy attempting an orbit. The old girl feels like she's on her last legs."

"Prop controls!" The engineer responded, picking up the landing checks.

"UP AND REVS ARE OK"

"Fuel...BOOSTER PUMPS ARE ON IN NUMBER TWO TANKS."

Adam had the flare path in his sights, now. The controls shook and jarred under his hands.

"Pilot to crew. This might be a bit bumpy,

chaps," he announced, laconically. "Hold on tight!" He switched off the intercom, twisted to speak to the engineer. "Ted!"

"Skipper?"

"As soon as we're down and rolling, cut all the switches. Whatever happens, cut all the switches!"

"Understood, Skipper."

"Navigator to pilot!" Ben called, over the open channel. "Leave out the three-point landing tonight, Skipper!"

Adam chuckled to himself.

Normally, he regarded it as a matter of honour to put a Lanc down on all three wheels, text book fashion. Hardly anybody did it nowadays. A three-point landing meant landing with a bare minimum of flying speed in reserve and in effect, stalling the kite onto the runway. Although he and Peter Tilliard regularly demonstrated the art, nobody else on the Squadron had even attempted it in his time at Ansham Wolds. It was one of too many ways to get yourself killed. Everybody else took the easy route; landing with an excess of speed and revs, flying, almost literally, onto the ground, getting the big main undercarriage wheels solidly planted on terra firma before chopping back the throttles and dropping the tail. That way if you misjudged your approach it was relatively easy to adjust once you were on the ground with a burst on one of the outer Merlins. Tonight, he would settle for any kind of landing that did not get them all killed.

"Pilot to navigator!" Adam retorted, ruefully, knowing he and his friend might well be exchanging their last words. In this life, at least. "I'll bear your recommendation in mind, old man!"

The High Wold was rising to meet L-Lincoln, the great chalk escarpment climbing up from the coastal plain. The Lancaster staggered drunkenly, lurched and reeled down an invisible stairway to the runway. Adam focussed on the flare path, fought the temptation to look to the left or the right, to look at anything other than his instruments and the beckoning airfield lights. He was exhausted, at the end of his tether physically and mentally. His muscles cried out, trembled with every exertion. He had been wrestling with the controls, fighting to keep the crippled bomber in the air for over three hours since the fighter attack. Over Holland he had contemplated ordering the chaps to bale out, seen no way of coaxing L-Lincoln across the cold, windswept barrier of the North Sea. Now came the moment of greatest peril. An instant's disorientation, a split second's lapse and the aircraft would stall, fall out of the sky. Suddenly, the ground was looming up – too fast - to embrace L-Lincoln. He steeled himself, kept the revs high, the Merlins surging.

The perimeter fence flashed beneath the nose, the dazzling, high-intensity gooseneck flares at the threshold stung his eyes. He held on as long as he dared, then delayed longer. At the last moment when it seemed as if the bomber was going to dash itself into the ground he hauled back on the controls and dumped the Lancaster heavily onto the wet tarmac. L-Lincoln's wheels hit the runway hard, squealed. The undercarriage took the strain, the airframe creaked ominously. Twenty tons of Lancaster bounced five feet, squashed down again. There was a loud CRACK from somewhere deep in the fuselage, the bomber groaned, then miraculously, settled on the runway and began to bump and roll.

"NO BRAKES!" Adam called.

"NO PRESSURE!" The engineer yelled back, already reaching for the cut-out switches, shutting off anything and everything which could hasten the onset of fire.

Adam chopped back the throttles.

The Merlins bellowed and subsided, their roar falling as the revs tumbled. The Lancaster skidded off the runway, onto the swampy infield. There was a dreadful, heart-stopping shudder as the bomber ploughed into the mire and L-Lincoln threatened to pitch forward onto her nose. Then she surged forward, headlong across the muddy field, spraying, churning sodden earth in her wake. The aircraft slowed, slowed as she rumbled onward, farther and farther away from the runway.

Coolly, deliberately Adam reached for the master engine cocks and selected OFF. Then, while the engines were still running he committed the cardinal sin of switching all eight ignition switches OFF. Wrecking Merlins went against the grain, but he seriously doubted that anybody was going to be using L-Lincoln's engines again. The Merlins spluttered and died, and L-Lincoln slid to a stop in the mud, hissing, creaking. Adam unbuckled his straps. The stench of 100-octane was over-powering.

"OUT! EVERYBODY OUT!" He screamed. This was not the time for niceties, nor the time to stand on one's dignity. "OUT!"

Pushing the engineer ahead of him he

clambered down through the fuselage. He was last out. Round Again, his fall cushioned by the quagmire underfoot, had dropped out of the nose hatch and was limping and hopping away on his sprained ankles. Ben splashed into the near distance with Taffy slung over his shoulder like a sack of potatoes. Bert Pound and Bob Marshall caught up with Round Again, each man grabbing one of the bomb-aimer's arms. Between them they picked up the young Scot and carried him away. Adam stumbled after them, dazed, ears ringing. Suddenly, waves of exhaustion washed over him and all he wanted to do was lie down and close his eyes.

The crew gathered in a huddle about fifty yards away from L-Lincoln. Fire engines, ambulances and a motley flotilla of other vehicles were approaching noisily, racing helter-skelter to be first on the scene.

"That," Ben remarked, breathlessly, sitting a sorry looking Taffy Davies down in a puddle. "Was a bloody awful landing, Skipper!"

Adam snorted, caught his breath and reached for his cigarette case. He patted his battledress pockets under his sheepskins. The cigarette case was nowhere to be found. It must have fallen out of his pocket in the excitement. He swore to himself, made as if to return to the bomber before he thought better of it. As if reading his mind Ben took hold of his elbow.

"I'll have a look in the morning," he told himself.

"Fucking awful landing!" Echoed Taffy, dazedly, trying to get to his feet, slipping, sliding helplessly in the mud. Ben let go of Adam's arm and placed a big, gentle paw on the gunner's shoulder to hold him down.

Adam sniffed. "So much for gratitude!" The others forced a laugh. "Anybody got any fags?" He inquired. "I seem to have mislaid mine."

The stench of 100-octane wafted over them.

"I thought I heard something break," Ted Hallowes commented, idly.

"Me, too," Ben concurred. There was a flash of flame, a small explosion. Suddenly fire was licking around the Lancaster.

"I think we might be a tad close for comfort, chaps," Adam observed, eying the burning bomber with the mild irritation of a man whose day had progressively gone from bad to worse and was unlikely to get much better.

Ben picked up Taffy and they started to walk away. Not in any particular hurry, but purposefully. Shortly afterwards, there was another, larger, louder and altogether more spectacular explosion. The hot breath of it rolled past them into the darkness and momentarily, night turned to day. One of the wing tanks had ignited. Nobody looked back.

Bert Pound lit up cigarettes as they trooped away from the wreck, and handed them round. Adam accepted the proffered smoke, inhaled deeply. He thought about Helen Fulshawe's cigarette case, lost somewhere in the flames.

And realised at last that he was free of Helen.

The past was gone, cleansed by the fires of the present.

Chapter 23

Saturday 22nd January, 1944
RAF Ansham Wolds, Lincolnshire

Adam shut the door of the Station Commander's office behind him, stood stiffly to attention before the big, polished desk and stared rigidly to his front. The rain drummed on the roof and pattered persistently against the windows. Otherwise, it was utterly quiet in the room.

They had watched L-Lincoln burning. Seven men smoking cigarettes bidding their farewells to ops. Another tour ended. It was not the ending they would have chosen but nevertheless, they had survived. They had watched the fires consume L-Lincoln like Vikings mourning the fiery death of a long ship, knowing that they would never fly together again as a crew. Adam had stared into the heart of the inferno, lost in his thoughts until Ben had nudged him in the ribs.

'Looks like the Groupie's on the warpath, Skipper!'

Adam had taken a last, long drag on his cigarette, tossed it away.

'You chaps cut along now,' he had told the others. 'I'll be along in a minute.'

There had been murder in Pat Farlane's face when he stumped up to Adam, breathing hard. A burning anger every bit as intense as the fires raging in the wreckage of L-Lincoln had blazed in his eyes. Adam had tried not to flinch, braced himself for the outburst. Pat had every right to tear him off a strip, bawl him out. But the explosion never happened.

The older man had gestured at his face.

'You're wounded?'

Adam had brushed his brow, become aware for the first time of the blood flowing freely down his face. The whole right side of his face felt numb, like he had been punched. In the excitement he had not noticed the injury, nor had he any recollection of how it had occurred.

'No, sir. It's nothing. I must have bashed into something when we baled out.'

'Get yourself patched up!'

'Yes, sir.'

'Report to my room at oh-nine-hundred.'

'Yes, sir!'

Adam would have felt better if Pat had put him out of his misery then and there. A swinging, haymaking right hook on the point of the jaw would, he suspected, have made them both feel a lot happier. Something summary, final. Something to draw a line under the affair. However, it was not to be. Adam had stopped off at the base hospital, got his scalp and left eyebrow stitched and bandaged, and later rejoined the rest of his crew minus Taffy to undergo the debriefing ritual.

Pat Farlane did not rise from his chair.

"How's that bolshie Welsh gunner?"

"Got a bit of a headache, sir. But apparently he's sitting up and taking nourishment." Adam reported, flatly.

"You look like you've been ten rounds with Joe Louis, yourself!"

"Yes, sir." The right side of Adam's face was puffy, mottled black and blue, sore and aching. Although the Flight Surgeon had stitched his gashed eyebrow back together with immense care, he did not look a pretty sight.

The Station Master sighed heavily, wearily.

"What will you tell Eleanor?"

Adam had anticipated a furious dressing down. He was not prepared for this. This was crueller by far. He judged it wise to say nothing.

"Or more to the point," Pat Farlane continued, slowly massaging the handlebars of his moustache between the thumb and index finger of his right hand. His voice was low, evenly modulated. "How do you think I'd have felt having to tell her you'd disobeyed orders and gone and got yourself killed? How do you think I'd have felt having to tell Eleanor that the man she loved was dead because the moment my back was turned he'd sneaked off on ops? That he was dead because he'd broken his word? That he'd got himself killed for nothing! Absolutely nothing!"

With anybody else Adam would have defended himself.

When he was silent, Pat went on.

"Well, you must have something to say for yourself?"

"No, sir."

His Station Commander grunted, levered himself upright and went to the window. He half-turned his back on the younger man, looked out across the windswept aerodrome.

"If you hadn't got back last night," he said softly, grimly. "About now, I'd be setting off to the village to tell Eleanor you were missing. So she didn't have to hear it from a stranger."

Adam swallowed hard, his throat suddenly very dry.

"In God's name!" Pat snapped, angrily, swinging around. "How on earth could you be such a clot, Adam?"

"Practice, sir."

The older man shook his head. "Practice!"

"Sorry, sir."

The Station Commander took a long, deep breath and sat down.

"I'm afraid it's a bit late for that," he retorted, bleak-eyed. "Somebody has already had a word in the Deputy AOC's shell-like about your little jaunt. No names, no pack drill but it was probably one of Freddie Tomlinson's people. For the record, Freddie's dreadfully upset about it. He rang me up at the crack of dawn to apologise. The poor fellow was absolutely mortified. He thinks you're a clot, too, but he was as keen as me to keep the lid on this thing. Unfortunately, the damage has been done. The long and the short of it is that an hour ago I got a call from the AOC."

"Oh," Adam winced. "I see."

Pat leaned towards him.

"You can forget about Messingham Priory." With a sinking heart Adam realised that there was more to come. "Ben Hardiman and the other members of your crew are to be posted off the station not later than twelve hundred hours tomorrow. At that hour you will present yourself to the Deputy AOC at Bawtry Hall when the subject of your future employment will be discussed.

Needless to say, whatever that employment may be it is unlikely to be in One Group!"

Pat Farlane dismissed him coldly, sadly.

"That will be all."

Adam stood there, rooted to the spot.

"Just get out!" The Station Commander barked. "Get out!"

Adam stumbled out of the room, returned to his billet and asked his batman, Crawford to pack his kit and belongings. It seemed a sensible precaution. Until last night Ben, Ted Hallowes and Bert Pound had been pencilled in for posting to 1671 HCU as instructors. Round Again and the gunners were off to other OTUs. Now there were new arrangements to be made and Adam sought out the Adjutant. He found him walking Rufus beyond the watchtower.

"Oh dear," Tom Villiers, frowned. "You really have been in the wars, sir."

Adam smiled, painfully. Rufus loped over to greet his master, who slapped him energetically, and stooped to let the dog lick the undamaged side of his face. In the distance the salvage crew clambered through the gutted carcass of L-Lincoln.

"I'm to go up to Group tomorrow," he informed the Adjutant. "I'd be obliged more than somewhat if you wouldn't mind taking charge of this old wolf until I know what's what?"

"Of course. I'd be delighted to, sir." The older man pursed his lips, lapsed into the role of the country solicitor that he once was, and yearned to be again. "Forgive me for asking, but has there been a change of plan? I understood things were, well, settled, sir?"

Adam wrestled Rufus aside and struggled to his feet.

"I'm afraid I rather blotted my copybook last night, Tom."

"Oh." Villiers was none the wiser. "I'm not sure I'm with you, sir?"

"I shouldn't have been flying last night."

"Ah," murmured the other man. "I didn't realise."

"Anyway, if you could look after the faithful hound until I find out how many lines the AOC sets me, I'd be much obliged, Tom."

"Skipper!" Called Ted Hallowes, catching up with Adam as he crossed the road outside the Mess on his way back to his quarters. "Skipper!" He panted, catching up with him. His head was as swathed in bandages as his pilot's but the lower part of his face was unmarked. "The Nav Leader says we've all been posted, Skipper?"

Adam stopped in his tracks, met his engineer's eye.

"Afraid so, Ted."

Hallowes recovered his breath, nodded.

"Because of last night, I suppose?"

"Yes."

The other man shrugged, smiled broadly.

"It was worth it, Skipper!" He declared defiantly. "We all knew last night was your century, Skipper."

Adam stared at him.

He ought to have told the chaps but after the way things turned out last night he had not had the heart. He had almost got them all killed and for what? Vanity? His stupid, schoolboy vanity?

"I didn't think anybody knew," he confessed, with a shrug.

Ted Hallowes grinned crookedly. He looked every bit as bruised and bloodied as his CO.

"The whole Squadron knew, Skipper! Oldest old lag to the newest sprog. Worst kept secret in One Group, Skipper!" The Flight Engineer said it with a no little relish, proudly.

"I see..."

"We wouldn't have missed it for the world, Skipper!" The other man was bouncing on his toes, unable to keep still. "If any of us hadn't been up for the op last night there was a queue of chaps a mile long itching to join the party. A hundred ops! That's a thing to tell your grandchildren, don't you think, Skipper?"

Adam did not know what to say. He blurted: "Sorry about Messingham Priory."

"Easy come, easy go, Skipper," Hallowes assured him. "Ben's organising a do in the Mess tonight. Should be a wizard party."

"A wizard party," Adam echoed. "I might be late, Ted. Don't wait for me. Start without me, okay?"

The other man gave him a thoughtful look.

"Okay, Skipper," he acknowledged, quietly. "We'll see you later, then?"

"Yes. Later."

Chapter 24

Saturday 22nd January, 1944
Ansham Hall, Ansham Wolds, Lincolnshire

Nobody was at home at the Gatekeeper's Lodge, so Adam had parked the Bentley and walked up the overgrown driveway to the ruins of Ansham Hall. He assumed that Eleanor and the children were at the Rectory and much as he longed to be with them, he could not face the Rector and his wife. Simon Naismith-Parry would want to debate with him, Adelaide would want to witter on about this and that. They meant well but today he was in no mood for the normal civilities, for polite small talk. He walked up onto the masonry-strewn terrace below the ruined house, sat on a low wall and lit a cigarette. It felt odd, retrieving a cigarette from a cardboard pack. He missed the feel of cold silver in his palm, thought idly about Helen Fulshawe's cigarette case lying scorched, misshapen somewhere in the wreckage of L-Lincoln.

A gusting, north easterly wind was blowing up the valley. The rain had relented, the skies were brightening. If the Magdeburg raid had been a costly failure for the Lancaster Force, it had been an unmitigated disaster for the Halifaxes. Once again they had borne the brunt of the fighter attacks. Inside twenty-four hours - in just two raids, against Berlin and Magdeburg - the fighters had shot down a quarter of the Halifax Force. Set against carnage on that scale Ansham Wolds' woes shrank into relative insignificance.

Nevertheless, 647 Squadron's woes were worthy of note. If only because they were typical of the woes of the majority of the squadrons of the Lancaster Force. Last night Peter Tilliard had loaned O-Orange to Jan van der Merwe, a South African with a sprog crew on the third operation of his second Lancaster tour: O-Orange had failed to return from Magdeburg, bringing the month's butcher's bill to 9 aircraft and 8 crews. Other than Peter Tilliard, only Ray Calder, the Worcestershire farmer's son who had inherited A Flight from Henry Barlow, survived of the pilots who were on the Squadron the day Adam had arrived at Ansham Wolds. Mac and a handful of men had transferred to Pathfinders or to other squadrons. The rest were gone, only their ghosts remained; victims of the winter war with the distant cities.

A Lancaster droned across the bottom of the valley, down towards Thurlby. Probably sprogs following the railway lines down to Brigg and the flatlands to the south around Gainsborough.

"Darling!"

Adam looked around to see Eleanor picking her way up the hill. She was dressed in dark slacks and an old woollen sweater, her hair streaming in the wind. He stood up, waved. She smiled and waved back, and danced up the steps to the terrace.

"My, my! You have been in the wars, haven't you, darling," she murmured, frowning her concern. "Ben warned me you were a bit of a sight!"

"Did he indeed!"

"I met him half-an-hour ago in the village,"

Eleanor explained.

"Oh." Adam muttered, feeling inordinately foolish. He wondered what else Ben had told her. "What have you done with Johnny and Emmy?"

"They've gone to Dennis Chester's birthday party at the Bowmans."

"Oh, I see."

"Have you been waiting long?"

"No, not long."

"I walked the children down to the Sherwood Arms at lunchtime." Eleanor was viewing him with rueful amusement. "I think we've forgotten something, don't you?"

"What's that?" He asked, like an idiot.

"This," she breathed, stepping up to him and cautiously extending her arms around his neck. She drew his bruised face down to hers and kissed him gently, warmly.

He hugged her tightly, momentarily lifting her off her feet.

"I thought you might be up at the Rectory," he told her, as they walked hand in hand through the woods to the Gatekeeper's Lodge.

"Oh, no. Not today. I'm afraid Simon and I had words, yesterday."

"Oh, I'm sorry to hear that."

"Simon's a good old stick, really. But sometimes he can be so infuriating. It'll be all right, but I shall leave it at least a day before I make a peace offering."

"What on earth did you have words about?" The man inquired. Their feet squelched through the sodden leaf cover, the wind plucked at the naked branches overhead beneath grey, scudding clouds.

"Well," Eleanor prefaced, her tone low, confidential. "I was talking with Betty Bowman, about today's party, actually. And she happened to mention in conversation, as one does, how disappointed Nancy, her niece was, not to have been able to marry Jack Gordon in church. Anyway, not knowing any better I asked why the wedding wasn't in St. Paul's. Poor Betty, she was so embarrassed. I think she felt she was talking out of turn. But in the end she told me the whole story. Apparently, when Simon found out about Nancy's 'condition' he refused point blank to marry her in St. Paul's."

"Her condition?"

"She was with child, darling," the woman whispered. "Somewhat out of wedlock, as it were."

"Oh."

"I went straight round to the Rectory and gave Simon a piece of my mind. Nancy's a good girl and the Bowmans are pillars of the community, decent, lovely people. I told Simon in no uncertain terms that the Christian thing to do would have been to turn a blind eye!"

"What did he say?"

"He was a little pompous and rather patronising. Basically, he didn't feel it was something I ought to be worrying my pretty little head about. I'm afraid I lost my temper. You'll think I'm wicked, but I asked him if Nancy Bowman's and my position had been reversed whether he would have treated me the same way as he treated Nancy Bowman." Adam tried and failed to imagine the look on the Reverend Naismith-

Parry's face at this juncture. It must have been a picture to behold. "He didn't know what to say to that," Eleanor went on. "I think he was too shocked to say anything. He went off in a huff and locked himself in his study!"

"Oh dear. Do you think he'll come out in time for next Saturday?"

"I do hope so, darling!"

They turned onto the muddy path which led behind the cottage. Eleanor unlatched the gate and they trudged through into the walled garden. At the kitchen door she stopped, planted a fond, pecking kiss on his good cheek.

"If you'd like to do something about the fire in the parlour, darling," Eleanor suggested. "I'll put the kettle on. Would you like scones? I made a batch for the children's party and kept back half-a-dozen for a special occasion. I think having you to myself on a Saturday afternoon counts as a special occasion. Don't you?"

Adam busied himself with setting the fire. Last night he had been fighting for his life over Germany, hundreds of miles from home and sanctuary: now he was looking forward to tea and scones with the woman he loved. He stared into the flames, transfixed, mesmerised. He saw heavies going down, multi-coloured TIs and Sky Markers falling into clouds stained blood red by the light of thousands of fires raging out of control in the streets below. The supersonic shock waves of countless cookies punched up into the clouds, blast waves rippled the undercast. He glanced to one side, saw a Lancaster disintegrate in a ball of red and white fire. In the distance blue-tinged tracer from a fighter's cannon arched across the night and lit up another anonymous heavy...

"Hello, remember me, darling?" Eleanor asked, kneeling beside him.

"Sorry," he grunted, dragging his eyes from the flames. "I was miles away."

"Like you were last night?"

So, she knew. He did not reply, sought refuge in the flames.

"Ben's an awful liar," Eleanor explained, matter of factly. "He said you'd walked into a door."

"In a manner of speaking, I did, actually. Walk into a door, I mean," Adam confessed, sheepishly. "I was in a dreadful funk at the time. The kite was pretty badly shot up. We were lucky to get it down in more or less one piece. I was convinced the kite was going to light up like a Roman candle any second. Seen it happen too often, I suppose. Bit careless, really."

The woman was silent.

Adam plucked up the courage to meet her gaze.

"Bit of a bad day at the office," he shrugged. She had a right to know what had happened. To know what manner of a fool she was due to marry one short week from now. "We got jumped by a fighter near Celle. Taffy didn't see it until it was almost too late. Luckily the other fellow must have been an absolute beginner or I wouldn't still be here to tell the tale. The silly sod almost collided with us. Anyway, I did my best to pull the wings off the kite shaking him off but not before the beggar shot away most of the rudders, and made a right old mess of the back end of the kite. The rear turret took at least two direct hits from twenty millimetre cannon shells. God only knows how Taffy got out of it with nothing worse than a nasty scalp wound. By rights we should have bought it. I could hardly steer the kite. No rudder, basically. Most of the rear elevators shot away. I couldn't keep her trimmed anywhere near level. She was flying like the tail wanted to fall off. I didn't think we'd get back across the North Sea. I'd have ordered the chaps to bale out over Holland if I'd thought they'd pay attention. Couldn't fly anything like a proper heading. It was like coming back from Wilhelmshaven all over again. Except this time it wasn't just me and Bert who were still alive. This time I knew if I made a mistake I was going to take six other chaps with me. All my fault. Honestly and truly, I have no idea how I got the kite down in one piece. There was no way of telling if the undercarriage was locked. No brakes. No way to keep the kite on the runway." He sighed a long, weary sigh. "So, as soon as we were on the ground we cut all the switches and baled out, sharpish. I didn't notice I'd whacked my head until Pat told me I was bleeding. The kite caught fire thirty seconds after we baled out. Bit of a shambles, really. Copybook comprehensively blotted, I'm afraid. Sorry."

Eleanor digested this unhurriedly.

She reached up and patted his chest just over his heart, and sighed.

"That settles it," she decided. "This definitely calls for scones."

Chapter 25

Sunday 23rd January, 1944
No. 1 Group Headquarters, Bawtry Hall, South Yorkshire

Adam had wasted neither time nor energy in the preparation of his defence. His was an open and shut case. He was guilty as charged. Moreover, other than regretting he had let down Pat Farlane he was thoroughly unrepentant. The deed was done. He had flown his hundredth op – his crews had celebrated most of the night – and he was still alive. He had confessed all to Eleanor and she had just smiled sympathetically. If the AOC wanted to make an example of him, so be it. No point worrying about it.

Cooling his heels in the anteroom outside the Deputy Group Commander's office his thoughts were far, far away. Around six the previous evening Eleanor and he had ventured out into the darkness to collect Johnny and Emmy. Eleanor had threaded her arm through his, leaned contentedly against him as they strolled. When he warned her that he was liable to be carpeted for flouting his screening she had pressed his hand.

'We'll worry about that if it happens, darling,' she commiserated. 'Whatever happens, we have each other.'

The back room of the Sherwood Arms was warm, noisy, and filled with children. Betty Bowman bustled hither and thither, red-faced, plump and smiling.

'Oh, Wing-Commander,' she exclaimed. 'Oh, we are so looking forward to the wedding. Oh, dear! What a nasty black eye! Still, it will have gone by this time next week, won't it. Do come in and meet everybody.'

Eleanor laughed and left him to his fate.

The birthday boy, Dennis Chester, was a large child for his seven years, with an unruly mop of fair hair and suspicious eyes whose initial brashness subsided into surprised, shy pleasure when Adam singled him out.

'Hello, Dennis. I gather you and Johnny are firm friends?'

'Yes, sir.' The boy stared at his stitched face, the fresh, puffy bruising.

'Ah, this?' Adam murmured rhetorically. 'We had a bit of a set to with a night fighter on the way to Magdeburg last night,' the hero said, grimacing for effect. 'Luckily we shook him off in the end.'

'Did you shoot him down?'

'Er, no. But then he didn't shoot us down either. So, I suppose it was what you'd call an honourable draw.'

'Were you shot?'

Adam chuckled. 'This? Goodness no. I got this walking into a door!'

Arnold Bowman, chortling good cheer stuck out a big, calloused hand.

'Good day to you, sir!' He boomed. 'Will you do me the honour of joining me in the snug for a pint, sir!'

Eleanor laughed, waved him to go with the publican. 'This is very civil of you, landlord,' Adam said, sipping a glass of the local warm, strong, flat ale. 'Just what I needed.' In his four months at Ansham Wolds he had never sampled the hospitality of the Sherwood Arms. An oversight he was glad to remedy.

'Your health, sir!' Toasted Arnold Bowman, raising his own mug. Presently, Eleanor put her head around the door, and cautiously entered the low, oak-beamed room. She was a regular visitor to the inn but rarely set foot in the public bar, or the snug. They were smoky, male domains. Places where she could not relax and in which she did not belong.

'Walking into a door, indeed!' She said, smiling a wan smile.

'Ah, there's a story to be told, I'll be bound!' Laughed Arnold Bowman, face lighting up with undisguised pleasure at Eleanor's entrance.

'Another day, perhaps,' Adam coloured as he stared into his beer. The Sherwood Arms might have existed in another world, a world that was totally divorced from the war being prosecuted by the denizens of Bawtry Hall...

That was yesterday, this was a new day.

Adam looked about the anteroom. The WAAF at the desk guarding the entrance to the Deputy AOC's lair inadvertently met his eye, half-smiled before she realised what she was doing. He grinned, ruefully rubbed his sore head. Last night Eleanor had bathed his face, daubed him with witch hazel to bring out the bruises. The result was that although this morning the damage looked a little worse it actually pained him much less.

'Keep still,' she had chided him. The ointment stung, he had wrinkled up his face. 'Don't be such a baby.' They were both a little light-headed by then. Once the children were in bed they had feasted on chicken broth, bread and a bottle of the Rector's peapod wine. 'There,' she giggled, stepping back. 'That should do the job, darling. You should be on your way. The others will be expecting you.'

'No, I don't think so.'

Eleanor had stood up, brushed herself down and regarded him fondly in the gloom of the single candle's flame. 'If you'd gone and got yourself killed last night, I'd have never, ever forgiven you. You know that, don't you?'

He had nodded, almost in contrition.

'Sorry.'

On the narrow landing outside the bedroom door he had picked her up in his arms, carried her inside and laid her across the bed. They had made love, slowly, intensely. Afterwards he had fallen into a deep, dreamless sleep. Awakening in the pre-dawn twilight Eleanor had been watching him, her brown eyes full of hope, sparkling bright.

'I hate appearances!' She had complained, curling up in the bed as he dressed, watching him sleepily.

'In a few days we won't have to worry about appearances,' he reminded her, pulling on his socks, casting around for his shoes.

'Oh, dear,' she moaned. 'I suppose I ought to apologise to Simon.'

'You may have been a tad hard on him. He's a good old stick, really.'

'I know, but sometimes he's so, so...'

'Old-fashioned?'

'Vexing!' She groaned, eyes laughing. 'Will I see you at Evensong?'

'I don't know.' He had bent over her, kissed her open mouth and furtively, like a burglar, slipped out of the cottage. It could have been in another world, another lifetime...

Adam glanced at the clock on the anteroom wall. It was nearly one o'clock. He got up, stepped across to the window. The rain had turned large areas of the construction site below the Hall into an impassable, abandoned quagmire. Workmen waded forlornly about the edges of the swamp. Behind him he heard the door open.

"Come in, Chantrey!" Adam marched into the big, airy room with its high, arched windows. Air Commodore Crowe-Martin did not take his seat, instead he halted before the younger man, eying him indignantly. "You're a damned troublemaker!" He rasped. "A damned troublemaker! What have you got to say for yourself?"

"Nothing, sir."

"Nothing, sir!"

"Other, than it seemed like a good idea at the time, sir."

"Did it?"

"Yes, sir. The last chance for a while to put up my century, sir."

"Yes. So I gather." The Deputy AOC turned on his heel, stalked around his broad, gleaming mahogany desk and dropped into his chair. A slim Manila file lay on his blotter. He opened it, scowling. Normally dapper and calm, today he was visibly agitated, tired and a little drawn, almost haggard, as if he had of late suffered one too many sleepless nights.

The repercussions of the Magdeburg disaster were reverberating around Bawtry Hall. The Group's squadrons were tired, the best crews exhausted. People were thinking the unthinkable, asking whether the Main Force had bitten off more than it could chew, even whispering that perhaps after all Berlin was too tough a nut to crack.

Crowe-Martin looked up, glaring at the younger man. "I have here Group Captain Farlane's after action report concerning Friday night's events. I do not propose to discuss the contents with you at this time. However, in the light of Group Captain Farlane's comments, and certain other, related considerations, the AOC has decided on this occasion, that further disciplinary action is inappropriate."

"I'm sorry, I don't understand, sir?"

"Suffice to say, that in the scale of things, the rights and wrongs of your actions, constitute small beer, Chantrey. Very small beer. However, the AOC has instructed me to warn you, in the most serious terms possible, as to your future conduct. On your return to Ansham Wolds you will report to Group Captain Farlane who has been apprised of the AOC's plans for your future employment. He will brief you accordingly."

With this said Adam was curtly, coldly dismissed. The younger man hesitated. Air Commodore Crowe-Martin's steely, unforgiving scrutiny affixed itself to his face.

"You're a bloody fool, Chantrey!"

"Yes, sir."

Chapter 26

Monday 24th January, 1944
The Gatekeeper's Lodge, Ansham Wolds, Lincolnshire

Adam had bolstered his failing courage with a stiff drink prior to setting off for the village. Hoping to catch Eleanor at the school he arrived to discover the building was already locked up, dark and empty. Wispy grey smoke rose from the chimney of the Gatekeeper's Lodge as he climbed out of the Bentley, and straightened his tunic. He tried not to look too grim. Eleanor opened the door and smiled. Her hair was tied back and she was wearing her old, frayed housecoat.

"Hello, darling. What a nice surprise," she said, happily.

They kissed quickly and she ushered him inside out of the cold. "I was just doing one or two chores," she told him. "Then I've promised to take the children up to the Rectory."

"Oh, right," he murmured. "I'm sorry about yesterday. Not making it to Evensong. When I got back from Group I got to talking with Pat, and what with one thing and another," he shrugged, guiltily. Pat had calmed down somewhat by the time he arrived back at the station. In fact his friend had been extraordinarily decent about the whole thing, all things considered. He had told Adam his fate, sympathised with him in the Mess over a pint. Then he had surrendered him to his crews and the party he had missed the previous evening which had spontaneously reconvened on his reappearance.

Subsequently, he had got very, very drunk.

"It doesn't matter, darling," Eleanor assured him. "Come through to the kitchen, the kettle is on."

Johnny and Emmy's voices carried in from the walled garden. Adam sat at the table.

"You're very quiet?" The woman prompted, gently concerned. "Is it such bad news?"

He looked up into her brown eyes, sighed. "No, not really."

Eleanor gazed at him. She tried to stay calm, told herself to be patient, and busied herself with the tea. Her hands trembled as she spooned tea into the pot from the battered old caddy, poured hot water on the leaves, fished out cups and saucers and put them on the table. She took off her housecoat, hung it by the door and sat down opposite the man.

"I take it you're not to be keel-hauled, after all?"

"No, not keel-hauled," he grinned, shamefaced. "I'm to be banished to the lost colony, presumably for the duration." His meaning did not immediately sink in and Eleanor stared at him blankly for a moment before the penny dropped.

"America!" She cried, half in disbelief.

"Washington, actually," he elaborated. "I'm to be seconded to something called the Joint Military Mission, or some such. It's all to do with Lend-Lease, and liaising with our colonial cousins. Haven't the foggiest idea what the Mission actually does. Pat says it's all about flying the flag and going to cocktail parties."

"But America, darling?"

"It's where the Chief sends his old lags, these days. To keep us out of mischief. To stop us flying ops."

"When do you leave?"

"I fly out on the fourteenth of next month." Adam's name was already pencilled in for a seat on the regular Liberator shuttle from Prestwick to New York via - depending on the weather - Reykjavik in Iceland, or Gander in Newfoundland.

"But that's only three weeks away."

"I'm to report to High Wycombe on the eleventh. Apparently, various people at the Air Ministry and the War Office need to see me before I set off. I get the impression that by the time I leave I'll be so genned up my head's liable to explode!"

Eleanor remembered to pour the tea. She was grateful for the opportunity to compose herself.

"I'm sorry," Adam muttered, haplessly.

"How long will you be away? Or haven't they said?"

"I don't know."

"Never mind."

Adam reached out across the table, took her hand in his. "You're taking this awfully well?"

"It's not as if it's your fault, darling," Eleanor replied, her cheerfulness forced. "It all sounds terribly exciting? America, Washington, the Military Mission? I just wish I was going with you."

"I wish you were coming, too."

They held hands across the table until it was time to go. Later, walking the children up the hill to the Rectory, Eleanor turned to him.

"I was thinking of asking Pat to give me away?"

She inquired, out of the blue.

Ben Hardiman had been posted to a desk job with Coastal Command in Londonderry. The rest of the crew had been dispersed to the farthest corners of Bomber Command. As Pat Farlane had remarked: 'the AOC takes a dim view of being made to look like a complete ass. Especially, when everybody else in Bomber Command wants to give you another medal for notching up your century!'

"Do you think he would?" She prompted, when Adam was slow to reply. "If we asked?"

"I think he would be extremely chuffed."

"He wouldn't think I was being forward?"

"No, not at all."

At the Rectory Adam paid his respects to the Naismith-Parry's and made good his escape, pleading the call of duty. Back at the station he stopped off at the Station Commander's office and mentioned Eleanor's suggestion to his friend.

"Be honoured!" Pat beamed. "Honoured!"

"That's settled, then."

Pat got up. "Let's go for a stroll. Give the old peg leg a bit of stick, what," he suggested, rapping his metal right leg just above the knee. They ambled down the corridor, collected Rufus from the Adjutant's room and headed slowly out towards the watchtower. "They're forecasting ops weather tomorrow," he remarked, cheerfully.

"You better put me under lock and key," Adam retorted, wryly.

"I might just, old son!"

Adam lit a cigarette, stared out across the darkened field. In the distance somebody was running up a Merlin. The latest forecast had generated a flurry of activity, a sudden urgency to get every available aircraft ready. "You never said what you put in your report to the AOC?"

"Oh, that." They walked on, past the watchtower and out along the perimeter road. In the stillness their leisurely footsteps rang out on the cold, damp tarmac. A stillness unbroken but for the faraway revving of the lonely Merlin in the night. On the other side of the aerodrome unseen, anonymous erks were toiling over their charge, watching pressures and temperatures, listening, trying to get the engine to run true. "I think what you did was pretty stupid, old son."

Adam nodded. It was meant well, without malice. He said nothing. There was nothing he could say.

Pat guffawed. "However, we'd be in a fine old pickle if we started cashiering chaps for pressing on, what! You simply can't go throwing the book at a chap for what, in effect, amounts to pressing on a hundred times. So, notwithstanding the fact that you're a prize clot, I decided it was in everybody's interests if I indicated to the AOC that I'd given you permission, informally, to fly the Magdeburg op. Just so you could bring up your hundred in style, as it were. The news is all round the Command, you know. You're quite the hero. That's probably why the Chief's so keen to send you off to the Americas to spread the gospel in the home of the free!"

Adam stopped dead in his tracks, too choked to reply.

Chapter 27

Wednesday 26th January, 1944
RAF Waltham Grange, Lincolnshire

The rain had stopped by the time the bus lurched to a halt outside the Waafery. Amidst the press of bodies, the shouted 'goodbyes', hurried last embraces, kisses and catcalls, Don McNeill disembarked with Suzy.

"You'll have to walk to the station if you don't jump back onboard, now," she warned him, lowly.

"It's not that far," he replied, smiling.

"Have it your own way." Suzy thought Don had a nice smile. The sort of smile that could easily distract a girl if she was in a mood to be distracted. She had half-suspected that Don had been put up to asking her out, possibly by the Wingco, or another member of his crew but the suspicion had soon waned as the evening progressed. The dapper, dark-eyed Canadian was very much his own man. In other circumstances she would have been flattered by his attentions, and very likely, let their situation resolve itself naturally.

"Okay. I don't mind if I do," he shrugged, unoffended.

Suzy's paper-thin mask of indifference split for a second. She giggled, lowered her eyes. Against all expectations she had enjoyed their 'date' in Lincoln. Instead of going to the cinema she had asked if they could go to a dance. That was safer, she decided. In the event the dance floor was packed and they had abandoned it early, walked and walked. Up the hill to the great Cathedral, down into the valley, along the banks of the River Witham, muddy grey and cold in the fading afternoon light. Contrary to her expectations, the CO's navigator had behaved like a perfect gentleman.

"So?" He asked, his voice almost drowned by the grating of the bus's gears. "Do I get a second chance?"

"A second chance?"

"Will you come out with me again?" The bus pulled away. Behind them a gaggle of WAAFs converged on the door to the Waafery, their voices carrying loudly.

"Look, Don," Suzy began, hesitantly. She hardly knew what to say, or how in truth, she really felt about him. "It's not that I don't like you, or anything. Or that I don't think we don't hit it off, because we do. Or at least, I think we do. It's just that, well, you know," she sighed, helplessly. "Things being the way they are. I don't want you to get the wrong idea about me, that's all."

He pursed his lips, remained silent.

"Oh, god. This sounds awful, I know," she apologised. "But anything could happen to you. You could be killed tomorrow. I know it is hard, but look at it from my point of view. If we were ever to get involved, I mean really involved, I'd go mad with worry every time you were on ops. I've gone through all that and I won't go through it again. Not ever."

The man lit a cigarette.

"So, was that a yes or a no?" He inquired, wryly.

"I suppose it was a yes and a no," she returned, uncomfortably. "I'd love to be your friend, Don. And to go out with you, now and then. But that's all. I'm sorry, but that's how it is."

The Canadian blew a smoke ring.

"Fair enough. Friends is good," he murmured. "You're right, of course. About being sensible, I mean."

"I'm sorry. Really, I am." Suzy stepped up to him, planted a frightened kiss on his cheek and fled inside the Waafery where there was a letter waiting in her pigeon hole. The envelope bore a Market Rasen post mark. It was from Margaret Warren.

The two women had promised to write to each other and had quickly fallen into the routine of exchanging letters every few days: Suzy with station gossip, and news about people Maggie knew, Maggie responding with news about her new life. Back in her room Suzy sat on her cot, broke open the envelope and unfolded the single sheet within.

North Farm, Tealby,
Lincolnshire

18th January, 1944.

Dear Suzy,

I was so sorry to hear about you and Peter. He seemed such a nice man but then I suppose some things are meant to be and some aren't. I'm a bit of a mess at the moment. Not really myself.

Harry is missing. The Brunswick show. His CO came to visit me. Gave me all the usual guff about how I shouldn't go giving up hope. He said lots of chaps get out when their kites go down. And that for all he knew Harry was safe and sound. The official telegram arrived this afternoon. I keep expecting Harry to come breezing through the door, throw down his cap and say "How's my English rose, today?"

I won't give up hope, of course. Until they tell me Harry's dead I shall carry on. They say I might not hear anything from the Red Cross for months, even if Harry is alive.

The funny thing is that although I've thought about what I would do when this happened pretty much from the moment I decided Harry was the man for me, nothing actually prepares you for how awful it is to suddenly realise that the man you love is gone.

I didn't think I would feel this helpless. If I didn't have the baby to think about I think I might give up.

Everybody's been very kind, people are always visiting. I haven't the heart to tell them that I would rather be alone. I know it sounds ungrateful, but I resent being the object of people's pity. It makes it harder to be strong and I know Harry would want me to be strong, now.

You mentioned you might visit North Farm in your last letter.

Do come up. I need somebody to cheer

me up.
Yours faithfully,
Maggie.

Suzy stared at the neat, evenly spaced script, and remembered the reports she had filed the morning after the Brunswick raid: of Lancasters blowing up in mid-air, of the wrecks of burning heavies on the ground signposting the way to the target. Then she thought about the wedding day photograph Maggie had shown her: the tall, handsome laughing Queenslander with his arm around his new wife's waist, and the serenity of the smile on Maggie's face. She sniffed, tears welled in her eyes, trickled down her cheeks, dripped onto the letter held in her numb, trembling hands. The words on the page began to blur.

It was so unfair, so cruel.

Chapter 28

Thursday 27th January, 1944
RAF Ansham Wolds, Lincolnshire

R-Robert rumbled up to the threshold. Bob Nicholson ran up the Merlins, throttled back in the gathering dusk. While the Halifax Force licked its wounds the Lancaster Force was on again for Berlin.

Adam stamped his feet in the cold and eyed the dark silhouettes of 647 Squadron's Lancasters lumbering, thundering around the perimeter road, navigation lights winking in the gloom as they queued for the off. The chorus of eighty-eight idling Merlins reverberated across the high wold. He envied Bob Nicholson, ached to be in his place even though he knew it could not be. He was no longer an ops man, his time at Ansham Wolds was over and he felt as if a part of him had been ripped out. A nagging, nameless emptiness doused his spirits. R-Robert was rolling. The crowd began to cheer and wave.

Adam straightened, saluted his successor as the bomber swept past.

"Good luck, Bob," he said privately, meaning it with all his heart.

Tonight for the first time, Bomber Command was despatching over 500 hundred Lancasters to the Big City. One bomber after another roared down the runway. It had started to rain and the heavies kicked up huge plumes of spray as they raced into the distance.

"I gather that America beckons, Wing-Commander?"

Adam half-turned, glanced at the Reverend Poore.

"Afraid so."

The Padre stood by his shoulder watching the Lancasters jockey for position, line up, gun their Merlins, pause briefly and then, hurl themselves forward. He always came out to see off the bombers. The dreadful thrill of the spectacle held him in its thrall. The names and faces of the men in the heavies changed, the roll of the dead, the missing and the maimed lengthened, the war became grimmer, more brutal by the day but still the Lancasters kept taking off.

"It won't be forever," the older man consoled him.

"I'm not convinced my wife-to-be sees it quite that way, Padre."

Q-Queenie's Merlins bellowed as she swept imperiously into the darkness. Q was Geoff Master's kite. Masters was Bob Nicholson's replacement as B Flight commander. Today was his twenty-second birthday.

"No, I suppose not."

Adam smiled to himself. Eleanor had not said as much, but deep down he knew she was relieved the RAF was spiriting him thousands of miles away. She understood that ops were in his soul and that if he was in England he would always yearn to be back on ops. For her sake if no other, he had decided to acquiesce to his secondment to Washington with good grace. Eleanor only wanted him to be safe from harm and he owed her that, at least. The war was not going to end tomorrow. In a few months he would be back. Back in England. Back in England and in the arms of the woman he loved, and most likely, back on ops, too.

T-Tommy lined up for takeoff.

"Do you remember what you said to me the first time we met, sir?" The Padre asked. "About atonement?"

"I do indeed."

"You told me that this was as good a place as any to atone? I've often thought about what you said that day. It made a very deep impression on me. Such an impression, in fact, that I've often wondered what prompted you to say what you said?"

T-Tommy's Merlins raced, the Lancaster surged forward.

"I suppose I wanted you to understand the way things are for us, Padre," Adam said, distractedly. "And that each of us has to make his own peace with it in his own way."

"And have you found a way?"

Adam shook his head.

"No, Padre. Not yet."

Epilogue

Sunday 17th December, 1944
North Farm, Tealby, Lincolnshire

Suzy watched the bus drive off, gears crashing, exhaust belching. Around her the High Wold seemed empty, desolate in the dusk of the winter afternoon. A fitful, cold wind blew off the North Sea, and clouds scudded across the darkening sky. The chill in the air spoke of a clear night to come, frost in the morning, and perhaps a dusting of snow; nothing that was likely to keep the Main Force at bay. She shivered, drew her greatcoat tight around her slender frame and picked up her bag.

Stepping between the murky grey puddles, carefully skirting the worst of the mud she made her way up the track, past the red brick tithe cottages towards the farm buildings. Land girls were billeted in the cottages, Maggie and little Harry had an upstairs room at the back of the big house. North Farm had once been a grand place. Now ivy covered the ramshackle Georgian mansion, hiding the cracks in its crumbling facade.

"Hello there!" Called a large woman in dungarees whom Suzy did not recognise from her previous visits. "It's Section Officer Mills, isn't it? You'll be looking for Maggie! She's in the office. She said for you to go straight through. Mind how you go in the yard, we brought the herd inside this morning."

"Thank you," Suzy waved. Since the spring she

had been a regular visitor to Tealby.

Her shoes were a mess, her stockings were splashed with mud, mire and worse before she reached the sanctuary of the broad stone step outside the door to the farm office. Not pausing, she went in.

A low fire was burning in the grate and the office was a picture of orderliness. Everything had its place and everything was in its place. The filing cabinet drawers were shut, shelves were stacked with papers and Ministry of Food Production publications, nothing was piled, nothing was heaped, nothing was lost, mislaid. Suzy heard the baby stirring, gurgling.

She put down her bag, went to the desk and peered over it.

Young Harry blinked at her sleepily from his bed in the big wicker basket. She smiled at the child, felt an immense urge to sweep him up in her arms. Each time she saw the baby she felt an unreasoning pang of jealousy. How she envied Maggie. And yet... And yet it had not been meant to be and it was no good dwelling on these things. Maggie had been lucky and she had not, there was nothing she could do about it. Nothing except carry on.

That was what Peter Tilliard would have wanted her to do.

Maggie had found her feet, got on with living and Suzy had decided from the outset that she could have no better example than Maggie Warren. Without her friend's shoulder to cry on she would have been utterly lost. Nothing disheartened Maggie, whatever the world threw at her she took it in her stride and carried on without a backward glance.

The old farmer, a man in his sixties had had a stroke in March, and been more or less bed-ridden ever since. Maggie had stepped in, first taking charge of the ever changing cadre of about a dozen or so land girls on the farm, and then the day to day running of the whole enterprise. She was a born organiser, the girls worked well for her and she had a light-touch with the men from the Ministry who had initially wanted to bring in an agent to manage North Farm. The arrangement suited everybody. The farmer and his family retained their home, North Farm remained in their name and Maggie was in her element. Her only worry was what would happen after the war but that still seemed somewhat academic, a prospect lying in an unknowable future and therefore, hardly worth worrying about. Suzy wished she shared her friend's unshakable belief that things would inevitably turn out for the best.

'Being a housewife is going to seem awfully dull after all this,' Maggie would observe, wryly. Otherwise, she seemed content, at peace with herself and her world.

Suzy heard the door creak behind her.

"Hello!" Maggie said cheerfully, hurrying in out of the cold.

Suzy turned around. Her friend was dressed in the same standard, coarse issue dungarees her girls wore, her hair, grown long since she had departed the Waafery, was tied back in a single haphazard pigtail. Maggie's cheeks were flushed and she was a little breathless.

"Things are a bit hectic," she explained. "We brought the herd inside, today."

"So I gather," Suzy grinned.

The two women hugged briefly and exchanged pecking kisses.

"Oh dear," Maggie exclaimed, "the mud, it's all over you!"

Suzy glanced down at her muddy feet.

"It'll sponge off."

They viewed each other in the rueful way they always looked at each other. They had been through so much in the last year, shared so much together that they were like sisters, united by their joys and travails.

"How are things at dear old Waltham Grange?"

"So, so," Suzy replied, guardedly, as was her wont of late. Then, remembering where she was and who she was talking to, she relaxed. "Lots of ops, but quiet, if you know what I mean. Not like in the old days."

"Oh, the old days!" Maggie laughed. "Aren't we a pair!"

"Aren't we," Suzy agreed. "Have you heard anything more from Harry?"

Maggie shook her head.

"No. Not since that letter in August."

"I suppose now the fighting's closer to Germany, the Red Cross can't get so many letters through the lines," Suzy sympathised.

"He's all right, that's all that matters."

Suzy's gaze settled momentarily on the wedding photograph on the big desk by the fire, Maggie laughing happily in the arms of the irrepressible Queenslander who had stolen her heart for ever.

Again, a pang of envy, and another of regret stabbed her to the heart. She dragged her eyes from the picture. A letter from the Red Cross in mid-March had confirmed that Harry Warren was alive and a prisoner of war in Germany.

"Every time I see little Harry I can't believe how much he's grown."

"I've sent Harry a picture. I don't know if it'll get through. But I thought I'd try, anyway." The two women stood over the baby for a moment. "Come through to the kitchen, you must be frozen," Maggie declared, clutching the handle of the basket.

They went outside, along the wet path around the back of North Farm. Soon they were settled at the kitchen table.

"I was terribly sorry to hear about Don," Maggie said, presently. She said it quietly, almost in passing.

Suzy pursed her lips.

"In a funny sort of way I was expecting it. Because it had been so long, I suppose."

Maggie nodded, poured the tea.

Clive Irving and his veteran crew had gone missing in an attack on the Nordstern synthetic oil plant at Gelsenkirchen in June. By rights Don McNeill ought to have been far away from Waltham Grange, far away from harm by then. He had flown the thirtieth op of his tour on a raid on Duisburg a month before but out of loyalty to Clive and the others had deferred his screening to allow the crew to complete its tour together. For the rest of the crew the attack had represented operation number twenty-nine.

Coming within six weeks of the news that Peter Tilliard was missing, Suzy had very nearly gone to pieces when Don had followed him into the night.

Maggie sat down opposite her friend.

"How are things, Suzy?" She asked, directly. "I don't mean at Waltham Grange, I mean with you?"

"I'm okay, really. Really I am."

Suzy stared into her tea.

Peter and his old friend, Clive Irving had briefly, been among the brightest stars in 1 Group's firmament. Both in their own very different, inimical ways had led their squadrons through and beyond the disasters of the spring. Both men had taken command in dire circumstances, both men had steered their respective ships through the rockiest of waters to the relative calm of the days following the end of the *Battle of Berlin*, as last winter's campaign had now been christened. Both were men who had inspired unquestioning loyalty in their crews, both had led from the front and both had died leading from the front.

In those grim days of February and March when every time the Main Force went to Germany it was terribly mauled, decimated, Peter had started flying as a passenger with his sprogs. 'To encourage the chaps, to make sure they know I'm on their side,' he told his old lags.

Peter had died flying with sprogs.

Killed on a Wednesday night at the beginning of May in the disastrous Lancaster Force raid on the Wehrmacht depot at Mailly-le-Camp, near Reims. It ought to have been a milk run, a massive, overwhelming attack on an undefended target only a few minutes flying time from the French coast that should have been over and done with long before the fighters had a chance to intervene. It was nobody's fault but something had gone horribly wrong and in the confusion the Luftwaffe had hacked down over 40 Lancasters. 1 Group alone had lost 27 aircraft that night.

Maggie, prompted by the rising thunder of Merlins from nearby Binbrook and sensing her friend's dark thoughts, got up and pulled the blackout blinds.

"They were flight testing this afternoon," she remarked, casually.

"Yes, I know."

"I wonder where it'll be tonight?"

Suzy sipped her tea. That autumn the Main Force had been turned against oil and transportation targets, but in between, it had resumed the onslaught against the German cities with a new and terrible ferocity. Of late casualties had been almost negligible. Now and then the weather took a hand and there were always the normal training crashes, but there were no 'big chop' nights, and very few nights at all when the defenders wrought anything worse than incidental, almost accidental casualties in the great bomber streams over Germany. By day and by night British and American bomber fleets now roamed at will across the German heartland, often completely unopposed.

Binbrook's Lancasters were taking off. The air trembled as the clamour of Merlins straining for height over Lincolnshire mounted towards its long, thunderous crescendo.

"Do you think Don understood how it was for

me?" Suzy asked suddenly, unsettling her host.

"About Peter, you mean?"

"Yes."

"I think so."

Suzy sniffed back her tears. Maggie reached out across the table, took her friend's hand in her own, pressed it gently. There were no words to say. No words that could begin to describe, let alone account for the madness and the tragedy of what was going on around them.

Binbrook's Lancasters were taking off.

Overhead the bombers climbed in the night, set their courses to the south and the east. In Germany winter snow cloaked the seas of rubble that had once been the sites of great cities. In England the ghosts of countless fresh-faced aircrew, many no more than boys, walked the windswept dispersals of a hundred Bomber Command airfields. And still the war went on. Both women were thinking the same thoughts, remembering alike the dead and the missing, the wounded and the broken, the desolation of waiting for aircraft that would never return, and the joy and relief of seeing again men who had survived another raid, another night.

Suzy looked up, tried to force a smile.

Maggie responded in kind. "Things will be all right, you'll see," she said, softly, defiantly. "Things will be all right."

Suzy nodded.

When she was low she always thought about Peter Tilliard.

He remained her strength, her protector against all ill and would forever more.

Monday 18th December, 1944
The Gatekeeper's Lodge, Ansham Wolds, Lincolnshire

Eleanor was rocking the cradle when Jonathan and Emily crept into the kitchen closely followed by Betty Bowman. Evening was drawing in over Lincolnshire on another wet, windy winter day. While the new baby held no fascination for Eleanor's son, his sister still peered into the cot with an intense, bewildered wonderment in her young eyes.

"She's just gone to sleep," Eleanor smiled, looking up.

"You keeping rocking her, my dear," Betty whispered. "While I get these two changed for tea."

Eleanor had learned not to argue with the older woman. These last few months the wife of the landlord of the Sherwood Arms had been a tower of strength. At first Eleanor was reluctant to ask for, let alone, accept help. She had imagined she could cope, make do, muddle through somehow and had never realised that so many people would actually want to help. Then the Rector had taken her to task, convinced her that she had to be sensible.

"You're wearing yourself out, Ellie," the old man had declared, putting on his sternest face. "And it won't do. It won't do at all! You must worry about yourself, now."

Betty Bowman had organised the women of the village to keep house for the Naismith-Parrys, and nursed Adelaide through her last illness. The Rector's wife had died the day after Hannah was born. The doctor thought it was a stroke; she had slipped away in her sleep, peacefully, quickly.

'Hannah?' Adelaide had asked only a few days before. The old lady had wanted to know what names she and Adam had discussed for the baby.

'Hannah Rachel if it's a girl,' Eleanor had explained. 'Paul Charles if it's a boy. Paul was Adam's brother's name, Charles for my father. It took us about a dozen letters before we made up our minds. And then we came back around to the names we had thought of in the beginning!'

'Hannah was your mother's name, of course?' Adelaide had not lived to set eyes on Eleanor's baby daughter. That was what hurt the most, it would have meant so much to her. It was odd how one small tragedy could seem so cruel in a world where tragedies without compare were an everyday occurrence.

"I'll put the kettle on, shall I?" Betty beamed, a large and reassuring presence as she bustled back into the kitchen.

Eleanor broke out of the circle of her thoughts. "I'm being terribly rude," she apologised. "Leaving everything to you like this, Betty."

"Don't you worry your pretty head about a thing, my dear," the older woman told her firmly. "You've got a lot on your mind."

Eleanor got to her feet. "You've been so kind to me," she sighed. "I don't know what I'd have done without your help."

"Nonsense, my dear. After everything you've done for the village. Taking on the school, looking after the Rector and his poor wife. Besides, what would the Group Captain think if we hadn't pitched in when you needed a little help? You tell me that!"

Eleanor gave in gracefully, let Betty carry on undisturbed.

Adam had been promoted acting-Group Captain in February to coincide with his arrival in America. Not that he had taken any real pleasure from it. He was too busy pining for home, and for ops: approximately in equal measure. Her husband viewed this latest promotion as no more or less than an unwanted obstacle barring his return to ops and his early letters were full of a quiet, understated frustration. It was partly to do with being separated from her so soon, but he was also angry to be on the sidelines, angry to be relegated to what he considered to be the backwater of the war.

Adam wrote long, lucid, marvellously eloquent, descriptive letters full of names, places, cogently argued opinions and anecdotes, punctuated with a wry, self-effacing humour. His letters were sometimes love letters, sometimes travelogues. Sometimes he wrote daily, and never less than three or four times a week. Everything came back to England uncensored via diplomatic couriers, some letters reaching her within the week. She had saved every letter, and now she had a thick sheaf of them. Browsing through his letters always lifted her spirits. She had taken to reading selected extracts out aloud for Johnny and Emmy. Much of it went over Emmy's head but Johnny listened closely.

Adam had travelled the length and breadth of North America talking to workers, journalists, speaking on the radio, meeting Congressmen and

Senators, attending parties, rallies, soirees, he had even been to Hollywood, met and dined with movie stars; all in the name of spreading the RAF gospel, talking a good war and flying the flag. He hated some of it. How he hated it! And yet no matter how he complained, she knew he secretly loved the travelling, the new sights, the great, booming cities of the United States; windy Chicago, winter bound Seattle, the shimmering summer heat of San Francisco, the skyscrapers of Manhattan. And most of all he loved the flying. Boeing, Consolidated, Douglas, Martin all wanted the handsome, bemedaled hero of a hundred bombing missions to sit at the controls of their aircraft and to wave to the photographers. He had flown all manner of aircraft, everything from a Mustang fighter to a brand new B-17 straight off the production line at Boeing's giant Seattle factory. In one of his recent letters he had described a flight in something called a 'Superfortress', over the Mohave Desert, which was in California, apparently.

Clearly, it had been a somewhat chastening experience.

'I looked over the pilot's shoulder and read the dials. We were at 27,000 feet, bowling along at 315 knots IAS, still climbing like a fighter, throttles nowhere near fully open. Sky azure blue from horizon to horizon, not a cloud. I was sitting in a pressurised cabin, warm enough for shirt-sleeves in the sun. Outside it was probably about minus thirty or forty. The chaps say they are sending five hundred of these

superforts out to the Pacific, maybe more. They're going to bomb Japan from Saipan and Guam. Compared to a Lanc or a B-17, these kites are pure Jules Verne. Huge, silver flying machines with bomb bays like hangars. Boeing claim that with all the stops pulled out, they can fly higher and faster than any Japanese fighter. God help the Japanese, that's all I can say! My word, we could have done with a few of these kites on our side of the pond last winter!'

Once he had found his feet, Adam had enjoyed America. Fallen head over heels in love with America, despite himself.

'Don't mope, darling,' Eleanor had written to him in April. 'You're safe where you are and that's all I care about. Make the best of it and keep safe.' That was the letter she had ended: 'PS. I am with child by thee.'

Whereas his letters rushed to her via official channels, her letters went back to him through the normal pedestrian, haphazard overseas mail. Frequently, her letters would not catch up with him for several weeks, and occasionally, they disappeared without trace. He did not receive the news that he was to be a father until the end of May. Thereafter, there was no more talk in his letters of 'wangling a quick return to ops'.

Bless him.

"He's safe," Eleanor reminded herself when she yearned to be with him. In the dark of the night she drew solace from memories of the blissful week they had spent as a family down in rainy Tavistock.

A week happily cooped up with Henrietta and her noisy, boisterous brood in the big house overlooking windswept Dartmoor. It had ended all too soon, in no time she and the children were alone again in the cottage. Alone with the pictures of the wedding. The whole village had turned out. It was like old times, a Grafton wedding was always the highlight of the year. Eleanor's wish had come true; she had got her white wedding and would cherish it forever. 647 Squadron's senior officers, led by Pat Farlane and Bob Nicholson had made an arch of swords outside the church for the newly-weds to duck through. The rain had held off, Adam's former crews - just returned from a gruelling overnight trip to Berlin - had packed St. Paul's, lined the path down the hill and cheered them on their way.

Eleanor missed Adam desperately.

The pain of separation was never far from the surface, always lurking to catch her unawares. Initially, Adam's secondment to the Joint Military Mission was for a six month period. This had seemed bad enough, but at least it meant he would be back in England in August, or September at the latest. Then, somebody at the Air Ministry had ordered an extension and Eleanor's hopes had been dashed. Adam was furious, but there was little he could do. He was so angry it prompted him to write promising that *'when this show is over we shan't ever be parted this way, again!'* He did not mean it, of course, and she had no intention of holding him to it.

Adam was half a world away in San Diego the day his daughter came into the world. Hannah was a small baby but the midwife had reassured Eleanor that for such an 'early' baby her daughter was strong and healthy. Jonathan and Emily had been small babies also, but Eleanor had not considered it politic to confide as much to the midwife. She had politely accepted the midwife's prognostication in the certain knowledge that Hannah's arrival was anything but 'early'. Secretly, she was proud of the fact that her new daughter was a love child, conceived almost certainly that first night she and Adam had slept together. It was right that Hannah was named for her own mother. Mother would have been proud of her, proud of both her daughter and granddaughter.

Hannah had been born on the evening of 6th October as the Lancasters of 647 Squadron took off, bound for Bremen. And so it was that the first sound her daughter had heard was the distant, rumbling thunder of Merlin engines in the night.

'Sort of appropriate,' Pat Farlane had remarked, visiting mother and daughter the next day. 'In a funny sort of way.'

'In a *very* funny sort of way,' Eleanor had agreed, ruefully.

Pat was a dear, dear man, and a good friend. Somebody she could talk to, and now and again, somebody upon whose shoulder she could cry. For his part, Pat welcomed her feminine company and the chance to relax away from the responsibilities of the station. He was a frequent visitor to the Gatekeeper's Lodge, once a month for a meal, weekly for high tea. He always made a fuss of the children, always cheered up their mother. To start with he had been wary of talking shop and steered well away from anything touching on his long, close friendship with Bert Fulshawe.

Then one day Eleanor had mentioned in a moment of devilment, that: 'Adam told me all about his affair with Helen.'

'Ah, I see,' Pat had stuttered, almost choking on his scone. 'Right, fine. Tricky subject, didn't want to tread on any toes. Look,' he added, uncomfortably. 'Dear old Bert thought the world of Adam. Between you and me, Bert and Helen weren't at all well matched. Chalk and cheese. What with the war and all, if it hadn't been Adam it would have been, and in fact probably was somebody else. Before and after the fact, I should add. Bert knew what Helen was like and that something was always going on behind his back. Helen would have rubbed his nose in it at some stage, I shouldn't wonder. In an odd sort of way I almost think Bert didn't mind. Not so long as it was only Adam. Better him than the chaps she'd, er, entertained before. And after, of course. Oh dear, this must sound absolutely awful. But you must understand that Bert and Adam were like brothers after the Wilhelmshaven show. After that afternoon we were all, I don't know, changed men. Bert and Adam even more than the rest of us, perhaps. The aircraft directly in front of them blew up, you know. They flew right through the explosion. An engine block, or some such went through the windscreen, caught Bert a glancing whack and took the poor old navigator's head clean off. Adam was unhurt. Bit shaken up, I daresay, but unhurt. Bert was out for the count, the kite was doing its best to fall out of the sky and it was getting dark. That was dicey in itself, we never used to fly at night, you see. Anyway, you get the picture. Rum do all round. Adam ended up following me back to Norfolk. Eventually he ditched on the beach at Southwold. Somehow. Fairly heroic stuff, in its way, especially in those days. After that, I always reckoned Bert felt he was in Adam's debt. A sort of debt of honour. What I'm trying to say is that Adam's affair with Helen had nothing to do with Bert's death. Bert was twitchy. He was twitchy and Helen was playing around with some Five Group type. His death was nothing to do with your Adam...'

647 Squadron's Lancasters had been in action again last night. The skies had throbbed with the heartbeat of bombers clawing for height over Lincolnshire. Hannah had slept through their return in the small hours of the morning; awakening only when the air was still and the land quiet.

"A nice cup of tea, then I shall be out of your way, my dear," Betty Bowman decided, fussing over Johnny and Emmy, settling them at the table. "Oh, did I tell you our Nancy's Jack is off to Pathfinders."

Eleanor said nothing. She did not trust herself to speak.

"I don't know what gets into them," Betty went on. "Men! I mean, Jack Gordon's done his bit. I don't know what's he's thinking of! What with Nancy and young Peter to think of. Nancy says he doesn't have to go back for another couple of months, yet."

Eleanor rocked the cradle, gazed at her daughter. Adam would be back on ops sometime in the New Year. It was inevitable. She would worry about it when the time came. For the present it was enough that any day now he would be back in England, in Lincolnshire with her and the children. They could start anew, contemplate a future together.

Perhaps as soon as today.

Adam's cable had been vague. *'I've managed to pull a few strings. Will be on the Pan Am Clipper Saturday or Sunday. With you next week. All my love...'* According to Pat the big flying boats took the Atlantic crossing in stages: Bermuda, the Azores, Lisbon, Southampton.

'Lucky beggar! Five-star service all the way over, what!'

Eleanor tried to keep her feet on the ground.

"The war will be over soon," she consoled Betty Bowman.

"But even so!"

"Things have changed," Eleanor soothed, smiling a wan smile. "Things aren't the way they were this time last year."

"No, thank goodness!"

A tour on Lancasters had long ago ceased to be a death sentence. Once in a while a squadron had a bad night, otherwise the temper of Bomber Command's war had changed out of all recognition. End of tour parties down at the Sherwood Arms were regular, almost weekly events, wakes few and far between. The long, bleak godless nightmare of last winter's campaign against Berlin was history. Thank God! Her Adam had been spared. God was good and had answered her prayers. Had Adam not been safe in America he could not have lived through those days. Mac, Bob Nicholson, Ray Calder, Geoff Masters, Peter Tilliard, even the indestructible Ben Hardiman, were gone. Eleanor had dutifully reported the news in her letters. All except the news about Ben.

'...Darling, you may already have heard, but Geoff Masters is missing. On last week's big raid on Frankfurt-am-Main...'

Adam would reply: *'Pity about Geoff, fine fellow...'* And leave it at that, there was little to be said. Eleanor had once asked him how he coped with losing so many friends.

'You can't dwell on these things,' was all he would say.

Bob Nicholson had gone missing in February on the Leipzig op - when 78 heavies had failed to return - one of three 647 Squadron casualties. Peter Tilliard had stepped into his shoes. Ray Calder, the affable, well-liked commander of A Flight and a staunch supporter of the Sherwood Arms, had been killed five nights later over Schweinfurt. Mac's Pathfinder Lancaster was shot down by a fighter on the way to Nuremburg; he had held the bomber steady while four of his crew baled out and then the aircraft had blown up. The Red Cross had sent news that Mac was buried at Ebensfeld, a village midway between Coburg and Bamberg, in Bavaria. In the aftermath of the Nuremburg disaster at the end of March - in which 95 heavies were shot down - Pat Farlane had confided to Eleanor that Bomber Command had lost more aircrew on that one night, than Fighter

Command had lost during the whole of the Battle of Britain. Having lost three Lancasters against Berlin earlier in that terrible week, 647 Squadron had lost another five that night.

Eight days before his death Kate McDonald had presented Mac with a son. Ewan Donald McDonald was a bright-eyed, lively baby, the light of his mother's young life, the son Mac had never laid eyes upon. Kate had sent Eleanor a picture of the child, and the two women corresponded most months. Mac's twenty-year-old widow was bearing up, coming to terms with life without the only man she had ever loved. Poor Kate.

Now Ben Hardiman was missing after a raid on Heilbronn a fortnight ago. The big man had visited Eleanor in September. He had despaired of Adam ever returning from 'across the pond', and was destined for 362 Squadron at Exton Manor, deep in 5 Group country. "I was going to hang around until Adam got back," Ben had told her. "But the way things are going if I don't get back on ops soon, it could be all over. I know he'll understand..."

Hannah gurgled, started to cry. Eleanor picked her up, rocked her in her arms. The baby stopped crying, stared up into her mother's face.

Eleanor heard the knock at the door.

Three knocks. Hard enough, loud enough to be heard in the kitchen without being heavy-handed, without being so loud as to cause alarm, or to give anybody inside a start. Her heart missed a beat, then raced. She had planned for this moment, played it over time and again in her mind. Yet all her carefully laid plans went out of the window in an instant.

Johnny rushed to the front door.

Eleanor heard the door open, voices in the hallway.

"Hello, young man," Adam said. "I hope you've been looking after your mother and your sisters?"

Eleanor turned, cradling Hannah in her arms.

Adam stood in the kitchen doorway.

[The End]

Author's End Note

Thank you for reading **After Midnight**. I hope you enjoyed it; if not, I am sorry. Either way, I still thank you for giving of your time and attention to read it. Civilisation depends on people like you.

Although all the events depicted in the narrative of **After Midnight** are set in a specific place and time the characters in it are the constructs of my own imagination. *Ansham Wolds, Waltham Grange, Kelmington* and *Faldwell* are fictional Bomber Command bases, likewise, *380, 388* and *647 Squadrons* exist only in my head. While *Bawtry Hall* was the Headquarters of No 1 Group, I have made no attempt to accurately depict it, or any members of the command staff posted to it in 1943 and 1944. Moreover, the words and actions attributed to specific officers at Bawtry Hall and elsewhere are *my* words.

One final thought.

A note on jargon. I have been at pains to make **After Midnight** accessible to readers who are relatively new to the subject matter and therefore not necessarily wholly conversant with the technologies and contemporary Royal Air Force 'service speak'; while attempting *not* to sacrifice the atmosphere and *reality* of that subject matter for readers who are already immersed in Bomber Command's campaigns. For example, I describe aircraft by employing their designated 'letters' –

that is, B-Baker, or T-Tommy and so on – rather than using the common RAF parlance of referring to an aircraft by its serial number. Likewise, where possible I look to explain technical terms and procedures in layperson's language. Inevitably, this leaves one open to the charge that one is 'dumbing down'; but there are many trade-offs in writing any serious work of fiction, and I sincerely hope I have drawn the line in more or less the right place. However, this is a judgement I leave to you, my reader.

Other Books by James Philip

The Timeline 10/27/62 World

The Timeline 10/27/62 - Main Series

Book 1: Operation Anadyr
Book 2: Love is Strange
Book 3: The Pillars of Hercules
Book 4: Red Dawn
Book 5: The Burning Time
Book 6: Tales of Brave Ulysses
Book 7: A Line in the Sand
Book 8: The Mountains of the Moon
Book 9: All Along the Watchtower
Book 10: Crow on the Cradle
Book 11: 1966 & All That

A standalone Timeline10/27/62 Novel

Football In The Ruins – The World Cup of 1966

Coming in 2018-19

Book12: Only In America
Book 13: Warsaw Concerto

Timeline 10/27/62 - USA

Book 1: Aftermath
Book 2: California Dreaming
Book 3: The Great Society
Book 4: Ask Not of Your Country
Book 5: The American Dream

Timeline 10/27/62 – Australia

Book 1: Cricket on the Beach
Book 2: Operation Manna

Other Series & Books

The Guy Winter Mysteries

Prologue: Winter's Pearl
Book 1: Winter's War
Book 2: Winter's Revenge
Book 3: Winter's Exile
Book 4: Winter's Return
Book 5: Winter's Spy
Book 6: Winter's Nemesis

The Harry Waters Series

Book 1: Islands of No Return
Book 2: Heroes
Book 3: Brothers in Arms

The Frankie Ransom Series

Book 1: A Ransom for Two Roses
Book 2: The Plains of Waterloo
Book 3: The Nantucket Sleighride

The Strangers Bureau Series

Book 1: Interlopers
Book 2: Pictures of Lily

NON-FICTION CRICKET BOOKS

FS Jackson
Lord Hawke

Audio Books of the following Titles are available (or are in production) now

Aftermath
After Midnight
A Ransom for Two Roses
Brothers in Arms
California Dreaming
Heroes
Islands of No Return
Love is Strange
Main Force Country
Operation Anadyr
The Big City
The Cloud Walkers
The Nantucket Sleighride
The Painter
The Pillars of Hercules
The Road to Berlin
The Plains of Waterloo
Until the Night
When Winter Comes
Winter's Exile
Winter's Nemesis
Winter's Pearl
Winter's Return
Winter's Revenge
Winter's Spy
Winter's War

Cricket Books edited by James Philip

The James D. Coldham Series
[Edited by James Philip]

Books

Northamptonshire Cricket: A History [1741-1958]
Lord Harris

Anthologies

Volume 1: Notes & Articles
Volume 2: Monographs No. 1 to 8

Monographs

No. 1 - William Brockwell
No. 2 - German Cricket
No. 3 - Devon Cricket
No. 4 - R.S. Holmes
No. 5 - Collectors & Collecting
No. 6 - Early Cricket Reporters
No. 7 – Northamptonshire
No. 8 - Cricket & Authors

Details of all James Philip's books and forthcoming publications
will be found on his website www.jamesphilip.co.uk

Cover artwork concepts by James Philip
Graphic Design by Beastleigh Web Design

Printed in Poland
by Amazon Fulfillment
Poland Sp. z o.o., Wrocław